H[illegible]er courage failed her. She was utterly miserable. 'I d[illegible]n't know. I just wonder what will happen next.'

'[illegible]hat's simple. We shall have to go.' He was wilfully r[illegible]sunderstanding her. 'Your father has sent a man who u[illegible] to be a farmer; he came yesterday and he's here a[illegible] today. I expect he will take over.'

[illegible]e was near to tears. 'I'm sorry, Giles. I hope it v[illegible] work out like that. I don't think mother . . .' Her v[illegible] trailed off because she could not say what she w[illegible]d to say with any conviction.

[illegible]s regarded her with a steady gaze and, without r[illegible]; his voice, in the same monotone as before, he s[illegible]I don't want to talk about any of this, Julie, and I c[illegible]want to talk to you. I would rather you didn't come h[illegible]ny more.' He turned and went into the house, c[illegible]g the door behind him.

[illegible]e stood, looking at the closed door. In just a couple o[illegible]s it seemed that her whole world had fallen apart.

W.J. Burley lived near Newquay in Cornwall, and was a schoolmaster until he retired to concentrate on his writing. His many Wycliffe books include, most recently, *Wycliffe and the Guild of Nine*. He died in 2002.

By W.J. Burley

A Taste of Power
Three Toed Pussy
Death in Willow Pattern
Wycliffe and How To Kill a Cat
Wycliffe and the Guilt Edged Alibi
Wycliffe and Death in a Salubrious Place
Wycliffe and Death in Stanley Street
Wycliffe and the Pea Green Boat
Wycliffe and the School Bullies
The Schoolmaster
Wycliffe and the Scapegoat
The Sixth Day
Charles and Elizabeth
Wycliffe in Paul's Court
The House of Care
Wycliffe's Wild Goose Chase
Wycliffe and the Beales
Wycliffe and the Four Jacks
Wycliffe and the Quiet Virgin
Wycliffe and the Winsor Blue
Wycliffe and the Tangled Web
Wycliffe and the Cycle of Death
Wycliffe and the Dead Flautist
Wycliffe and the Last Rites
Wycliffe and the Dunes Mystery
Wycliffe and the House of Fear
Wycliffe and the Redhead
Wycliffe and the Guild of Nine

Wycliffe AND THE LAST RITES

W.J.Burley

An Orion paperback

First published in Great Britain in 1992
by Victor Gollancz Ltd
First published in paperback in 1993
by Corgi Books
This paperback edition published in 2017
by Orion Books
an imprint of The Orion Publishing Group Ltd,
Carmelite House, 50 Victoria Embankment,
London EC4Y 0DZ

An Hachette UK company

1 3 5 7 9 10 8 6 4 2

A CIP catalogue record for this book is
available from the British Library.

ISBN 978-1-4091-7469-1

Printed and bound in Great Britain by
Clays Ltd, St Ives plc

MIX
Paper from
responsible sources
FSC® C104740

www.orionbooks.co.uk

Chapter One

Wednesday

He came in from the bathroom, still naked, and reached for his briefs. Katherine, sitting up in bed, watched him dress. Geach was a big man – not tall, but powerfully built, rough hewn; his body surfaces seemed to consist of intersecting planes rather than curves. The tangle of hair on his chest was turning grey but his head was thatched with dark, tight little curls. He put on his shirt, socks and trousers and came to bend over her.

'All right?'

'I expect I'll live.'

He kissed her on the lips, then on her breasts. His features, like the rest of him, were on a generous scale; the skin of his face, free from any blemish, was coarse, lightly pitted like the skin of an orange. He was smiling, a little smile of self-content.

He went to the door, paused, and looked back. 'See you later!'

'I'll be down.'

'Don't bother; have a lie-in. Elsa will look after me.'

It was as though he had patted her on the head and said, 'You've done your bit.'

She remained in bed, motionless, staring at nothing. After sex with Abe she seemed to exist only by proxy, a reflection in a mirror. She was nothing, she felt nothing, she had nothing – not even a body that was hers.

Of course this was nonsense! Abe was no monster, and she was better off than most; she had a daughter; she had a home – an old house which she loved; a car for her own use . . . money, which she could spend without question . . . True, these things were contingent upon her being and remaining Mrs Abe Geach, but hadn't she settled for that?

'You don't know when you're well off!' Others would have told her, but there was no need. She told herself. But that was logic and she had never found much consolation in logic.

From the bed she could see herself in the mirror of the dressing table: one of Abe's contrived titillations. I am thirty-nine. Do I look it? Her hair was dark and lustrous; no sign of grey yet. Later she would go through that iron-grey phase which is supposed to make men look distinguished but delivers women to the sorcery of hairdressers. Well, she would have none of that. If it turned out that there was life after the menopause she had no intention of making herself ridiculous, fighting a rearguard action.

The pallor of her skin was accentuated by her dark hair and eyes. Johnny Glynn had said once, 'Your eyes are like minefields, Kathy – still, yet menacing.' Vintage Johnny Glynn, master of the slick phrase and the slicker lay. God! I mustn't start thinking of all that.

Watching herself in the mirror she ran her hands slowly through her hair, lifting its weight from her head and letting it slip back through her fingers.

Her twin sister, Jessica, had gone about things differently . . . She wondered about Jessica. Was she happier? Silly question. Was she content rather than resigned? Against all the odds it might be so. Two women, a man, and a teenage boy, trying to scrape a living out of a few acres with little real know-how between them.

In a sudden burst of restlessness Katherine got out of

bed and drew back the curtains. There it was, the scene that had become part of her: the lawn and the shrubbery, then the low, crumbling bank, a stretch of muddy shingle, and the creek. There were primroses in the hedge which separated them from the churchyard. Across the creek the little boatyard, with its shed and thicket of masts, stood out against the rising ground of Trennick Wood. The rusty iron roof of the old shed glowed red and orange in the sunlight. It was half-tide and gulls padded about the muddy margins. Perhaps it was the house she had married.

She put on her dressing gown and slippers, spent a few minutes in the bathroom, then went downstairs to the kitchen. They always breakfasted in the big, old-fashioned kitchen. Abe was finishing his second egg and there was a yellow smear on his chin. He had eaten two soft-boiled eggs for breakfast every morning since the age of thirteen, when his mother decided that male adolescents required special nourishment. Now, at forty-one, regardless of hazards from cholesterol and listeria, he clung to his eggs as an addict to his regular shot.

The wall clock showed ten minutes to eight. Kathy said, 'Julie not down yet? She'll be late for school.'

Abe looked at her in mild reproach. 'It's Wednesday; from today she's off school for the Easter holidays. You did know, Kath.'

Black mark. She should have remembered.

Elsa came in from the yard. 'Oh, you're down, Kathy. There's plenty of coffee in the pot.'

Elsa's position in the family was ambivalent, a sort of cousin who was also a sort of housekeeper. She was three years younger than Kathy, unmarried and childless, yet, in Kathy's eyes, she was the real woman of the two. One could hardly look at Elsa without being conscious of her plump body, her pink skin, and her freckled fairness. Did

Abe ever . . . ? Very likely; but Kathy had decided early on that there would be no friction on that score.

Kathy poured herself a cup of coffee; no sugar, but a dash of semi-skimmed.

Abe finished his second egg, drank his coffee, and said, 'I shall be in the site office for most of the day if you want me . . .'

Abe looked what he was, a prosperous builder, and he followed tradition in carrying on the family firm.

'Try to keep Julie away from the farm, and the Vinter boy.'

Kathy was irritated. 'I can't choose her friends for her and neither can you; she's seventeen.'

'You could try.'

As he spoke, Julie came in wearing a jade-green dressing gown over her nightdress. A slim, dark girl, her hair was tousled, her eyes puffed with sleep. She yawned, bracing her shoulders and stretching her arms. 'Any coffee going?'

Abe, briefcase in hand, was ready to go. 'Ah, there you are!' He pecked at his daughter's cheek, ruffled her hair, and said, 'Bye, kid! Have a good day, and keep away from young Vinter, he's a poof!'

'He's not a poof, Dad.' Julie's protest was mild.

'Well, if he isn't he's in training to be one.'

Julie produced a handkerchief from the pocket of her dressing gown, moistened it with her saliva, and wiped the egg from his chin. 'You are a mucky pup, Dad!'

She went with him out into the yard, to his car.

Elsa said, 'They make a good pair. She knows how to handle him, which is more than can be said for her mother. I bet she'll come back with a nice crisp tenner tucked in the pocket of her dressing gown.'

They heard Abe's car drive out of the yard and a moment or two later Julie came in with a handful of mail which she dropped beside Kathy's plate.

'I met the postman.' She stood, hesitating, then, 'I think I'll go up and get dressed. Then I'm going out – is that all right?'

'It's your holiday.'

The two women sat on, nibbling cold toast and sipping coffee. Elsa lit a cigarette.

Although Abe built houses with designer-everything, fingertip central heating and a proliferation of elegant plumbing, Trigg House itself was, in all these things, at least forty years behind the times. But that was how Kathy liked it. Above all there was this archaic kitchen with a great square table in the middle, reminding her of the farmhouse in which she had been brought up.

Julie came down dressed for the street: jeans and a T-shirt with an unreadable slogan. 'All right; I'm off. Don't worry if I'm not in for lunch . . . Bye!' She was gone.

Katherine's eyes followed her daughter. 'She's changed. I seem to be losing contact and it worries me sometimes.'

'She's growing up, Kath; she's a young woman.'

Katherine reached for another piece of toast, changed her mind, and pushed her plate away. 'Abe is right about young Vinter; I wish she would find somebody else.'

Elsa mumbled with her mouth full, 'You don't know when you're well off. At least he's safe. She's not going to turn up pregnant one day – not by him, anyway.'

Elsa cleared her mouth and reached for her coffee cup. 'By the way, I suppose you know that Jessica is working part-time for Arnold Paul?'

Kathy paused, her cup to her lips. 'What on earth is she doing there?'

'Housework, I suppose – what else? I gather things have got too much for the old housekeeper biddy now that Arnold has his brother there. I heard it in the shop yesterday but I thought you must know.'

Kathy put down her cup. 'I can't believe it!'

'I don't know why not; she's done the church cleaning for years.'

Kathy was tense. 'That's different. I wish to God she'd agree to sell the bloody farm. Abe's syndicate would pay through the nose and it's not as though she'll ever make a decent living from it.'

Elsa blew out a cloud of pale-grey smoke. 'Not with the hangers-on she's got there now, she won't. At least Jess is willing to work, I'll say that for her; I don't know how she fits it all in.'

Kathy was on her feet. 'I'm going upstairs to change. I shall have a word with Jessica.'

A quarter of an hour later Kathy came down, transformed; she wore a fine checked skirt, a silk blouse, suede jacket and shoes, all in matching shades of grey, set off by a jade necklace and earrings mounted in gold – Abe's Christmas present.

Elsa was appraising. 'You're taking the car?'

'No.'

'You're never walking along the river bank in those shoes?'

'I'm going round by the road.'

'I see. We want to bolster our courage. Anyway, don't blow your top when you get there; it won't do any good.'

The village square, junction of three roads, merged with the foreshore where boats were drawn up on the shingle. At spring tides, when the wind was right, there was sometimes flooding and none of the houses around the square was without its stock of sandbags, ready filled. Across from Trigg, the garage with its petrol pumps adjoined the boatyard, while pub, post office, general store, café and a few houses completed the square.

'Morning, Kathy!' Tommy Noall, at the garage, his head under the bonnet of a car. They had been at the village school together until the age of eleven. Henry Clemens, who kept the general store and post office, was washing down his shop front. 'Nice morning, Mrs Geach! Makes you think the good Lord has given us spring at last.' Henry was the churchwarden.

Kathy usually enjoyed walking through her village, knowing, and being known. She was still one of the Dobell twins but she was also Mrs Abe Geach, wife of the contractor who built quality housing, government offices and schools. At such moments it pleased her to be both, but the news about Jessica had put her off-balance.

She turned up Church Lane, which followed the Trigg boundary until it reached the churchyard. The trees, their leaves breaking out of bud, were misty green against the sky and, opposite the church, in the gardens of detached villas, there were camellias and magnolias in flower.

Another two or three hundred yards, and she was in open country, out of sight of the village. Only the church tower, with its four pinnacles and flag-pole, rose out of green fields to mark where the village lay. A ramshackle gate labelled 'Minions' gave on to a rutted track which ran through an area of scrub where tethered goats were browsing. The track dropped steeply between high hedges, to end at another gate and the farmyard where hens strutted and pecked over the cobbles. A house backed on the yard and there were outbuildings on two other sides. As always, the yard, the hens and the smells brought back her childhood with disturbing poignancy. Nothing had changed.

Minions had belonged to her parents, both killed in a coach crash in the early years of her marriage. Jessica had insisted on keeping the farm going, first with the help of paid labour, later with the doubtful assistance of a succession of lame ducks needing a roof over their heads. The latest and, so far, the most enduring of these, was a family of three: Laurence and Stephanie Vinter, and their son, Giles.

As Kathy unhooked the gate Jessica's collie came bounding out of the house, barking, but changed to tail wagging when he saw Kathy. The door led directly into the kitchen and Kathy went in without knocking. The boy, Giles, was seated at the kitchen table, his school books spread out in front of him. He was the same age as Julie and they were in the same form at school. Slim, and small and fair, with the delicate features and colouring of a girl, his eyes were an intense blue, accentuated by the powerful lenses of his spectacles.

'Oh, Mrs Geach!' His manner was precise and distant.

'Working in the holidays, Giles? I wish Julie would. What subjects are you doing for your A-levels? Physics, chemistry and biology – the same as Julie, isn't it?'

'I'm doing mathematics instead of biology.' Giles glanced down at his books and back again. 'You want to see Miss Jessica? I think she's mucking out the goat house.' The blue eyes blinked at her and she realized that she was being dismissed.

She found Jessica manhandling a bale of bedding-straw into the goat house.

'Kathy! Let me dump this and we'll go indoors.'

They were twins, but no more alike than most sisters. Jessica was more sturdily built; her hair and eyes were less dark, her skin was lightly tanned, and her expression more open. She had a ready smile. In her denim blouse and jeans, her hair caught back with a clip, she seemed to typify the modern working woman in a way that Kathy had no desire to emulate but envied all the same.

The bale disposed of, Jessica came out of the goat house brushing herself off. She surveyed her sister. 'You look like an advertisement in *Country Life*, Kath! Those shoes haven't been along the river bank. Where's the car?'

'I walked round by the road.' Katherine was terse.

'Oh, I see; giving the peasants a treat.'

In the kitchen Jessica spoke sharply to the boy, 'There's straw in the goat house that needs spreading, Giles. Don't use it all; there's enough for tomorrow as well.'

Giles got up without a word and went out into the yard. 'That boy would never get off his backside unless I chivvied him . . . Gets it from his mother. Come into the sitting room . . .'

Kathy said, 'I thought Julie might have been here.'

'She was, but it seems his highness wasn't in the mood for dalliance. They chatted for a few minutes then she was dismissed. Everybody to their taste but I don't know what she sees in him.'

The house fronted on an inlet from the river overhung by trees, and the tiny window of the sitting room let in a dim and sombre light. Little had changed here over the years except by wear and tear; the black leather sofa, the armchairs, his and hers, the coloured prints in gilded frames, the upright piano against one wall – all had been there when the girls were born in the room above. So had the roll-topped desk and the wooden filing box which successive Dobells had used for their farm records and accounts.

'Take the weight off your feet, Kath. Feel like a sherry? To be precise, do you feel like risking my fortified wine which I now buy in five-litre plastic containers? I serve it from a sherry bottle but it might taste better from an old boot.'

The two sisters sat, side-by-side on the sofa, sipping fortified wine. 'Where are Laurence and Stephanie?'

'Laurence is out digging potatoes. As for Stephanie, it's the first day of the curse so she won't put in an appearance till mid-morning.' Jessica sighed. 'And lately she's taken to having afternoons off. Where she goes, God knows, but

I notice she's having more baths than she used to.'

'But if they're no use, why do you put up with them, Jess?'

Jessica poured herself a little more wine. 'Top you up? . . . No? . . . Oh, I don't know! I can't get anybody else and though Laurence isn't God's gift as a farm labourer, he works hard at whatever you tell him to do.' Jessica grinned. 'And he's got other attributes – of a sort.'

Katherine looked at her sister. 'I hope you don't mean what I think you do.'

Jessica's laugh had in it a strain of bitterness. 'You're an old prude, Kath! Sometimes I think you've turned being a woman into a career – like you took a course or read it in a textbook.'

Katherine was piqued. 'And what have you done?'

Jessica emptied her glass. 'Me? I don't know – what comes naturally, I suppose.' She was suddenly serious. 'If I've done nothing else I've plucked the feathers from a few cockerels and put a stop to their crowing – and I'm not dependent on any one of the bastards.'

'And I am? You might as well say it. But don't let's get into an argument. If you agreed, we could sell this place to the syndicate. You'd get a good price for your share and you could insist on a stake in whatever they made of it. You'd be well off, and still your own woman.'

But Jessica was indignant. 'Not on your life! If you've come here to push Abe's barrow, you're wasting your precious time. If I give up here it won't be for what I can get. Billy Eva would like to add it to his holding; then, at least, it would stay as a farm. As it is, I sell all I can grow, there's a steady demand for the goats' milk, and Billy is going to rent Five-acre for his store cattle . . . All that, with what I get from the church, and now from Arnold Paul—'

'That's another thing, Jess – I've just heard about it.'

'So? It's only two afternoons a week and the money's good.'

'But it's charring, Jess!'

'So what? I've been keeping the church clean for years.'

'But that's different . . .'

'Why? Because people might be daft enough to think I do it for love? Really, Kath!'

As always, in her encounters with her sister, Kathy was outmanoeuvred and made to feel naive and snobbish. It was she who changed the subject.

'I was saying to Elsa, I'm a bit worried about Julie; she's been seeing a lot of Giles lately.'

Jessica's reaction was similar to Elsa's. 'At least she's safe with him – no drugs, and not much sex either if I'm any judge.'

'What do they do when she comes here?'

'Sometimes they go out bird-watching but mostly they stay up in his room. For God's sake, Kath; they're seventeen! All the same, I wouldn't be surprised if they spend the time doing their homework.'

Jessica broke off and became solemn again. It was as though she had waited for a chance to turn the conversation her way. 'Kath, did you see in the local rag that Mrs Ruse – Derek's mother, is dead?'

'Ruse? The mother of the boy killed in the hit-and-run – yes, I saw an account of her funeral. What about it?'

'She was only fifty-five and they say she never got over Derek's death. After sixteen years she was still grieving . . .'

'So?'

Jessica was silent for a while, then she said, 'I was going around with Johnny Glynn at that time.'

'Everybody thought you would marry him – me included.'

'It was all fixed, and it was what happened that night which put an end to it.'

'But Johnny satisfied the police he wasn't involved. Of course, not everybody believed him.'

'I know they didn't, but he was telling the truth.'

Katherine looked at her sister. 'If Johnny wasn't there, who was?' Her manner became more intense. 'Jess, were you with him, whoever he was?'

Jessica made a sudden movement. 'I'm being morbid, Kath. Forget it! Let's talk about you. I hear Abe's got the contract for the new school up Liskeard way . . . I hope he's going to live long enough to enjoy it all – not like his father.'

Good Friday

'Almighty God, we beseech thee graciously to behold this thy family, for which our Lord Jesus Christ was contented to be betrayed . . .'

The Reverend Michael Jordan, Vicar of Moresk, in his high-pitched, boyish voice, recited the first collect for the day to a congregation that filled his church.

By some quirk of tradition the Good Friday morning service had acquired a significance for many villagers who were unlikely to be seen in church at any other time. The occasion was signalled, shortly before half past nine in the morning, by a stroke on the tenor bell to be repeated at one-minute intervals until the service began at ten. Each stroke marked a year in the thirty-three years of Christ's life on earth.

The morning was fine and sunlight streamed through a south window to fall dramatically on a larger-than-life statue of the Christ, set at the top of the chancel steps.

It was a family occasion; the Geaches were there,

occupying a pew halfway down the central aisle. Abe, out of his element, was flushed, as though he had fortified himself beforehand. He fumbled the responses and was unsure when to sit or stand. Even Jessica, who rarely attended a service, sat next to Julie on the inside. Kathy, in a hat that she kept for funerals, looked about her and realized that hers was one of less than a score of hats in the congregation, and those were largely confined to women whom she regarded as church hens.

'We will sing the hymn, "O sacred head, sore wounded, Defiled and put to scorn . . ." Verses three and four will be taken as a solo.'

Arnold Paul, at the organ, reached his high point in a composition of his own: 'Chorale Prelude by Arnold Paul, in the manner of J. S. Bach'; a lengthy introduction to the hymn based on Hassler's melody.

Kathy was watching her daughter who seemed to have eyes only for Giles Vinter. The boy sat with his parents in the pew in front; he faced straight ahead, as though unaware of anyone else in the church, and followed precisely the requirements of the ritual. She asked herself again, what did Julie see in him? Surely it was natural for a young girl to be attracted by masculinity? But there was nothing macho about Giles. On the contrary he was half a head shorter than Julie, his appearance was effeminate, and his short-sightedness caused him to peer like a cartoon professor. Of course he had more than his ration of brains, but when had brains stirred the hormones of youth?

Paul's prelude came to an end and a chord brought the congregation to its feet. For no obvious reason Kathy felt vaguely depressed and apprehensive. Her sensations were similar to those she often experienced at the approach of a thunderstorm, when the atmosphere itself seemed permeated by some undefined menace. She wondered if she might be on the brink of an illness.

To her surprise the solo was taken by Stephanie Vinter from her place in the congregation. Kathy was impressed. Stephanie's unaccompanied soprano had a bell-like sweetness, a magical quality which suspended normality and, when the organ brought in the congregation for the final verse, it was as though everyone drew breath again. During her solo Giles had watched his mother with total absorption and seemed to live with her through every moment of the experience.

The congregation knelt. 'Almighty and everlasting God, by whose Spirit the whole body of the Church is governed . . .'

Laurence Vinter, his head bowed low, studied the grain of the bookrest. For weeks he had lived with a growing sense of unease and tension. He could point to no significant change in the daily life of the farm, nor in their relationships, yet he was conscious of an impending crisis.

As each day passed it seemed that their words became overloaded with meaning, that their simplest actions might be fraught with sinister implications. At times he felt that he was picking his way along a crumbling traverse, and his concern was not lessened by his inability to decide whether the crisis was real or, as he often suspected, a creation of his own disordered mind.

Another hymn, and towards the end of it the vicar ascended the steps to his pulpit.

'My text is taken from Isaiah, chapter 53, verse 3: "He was despised, and we esteemed him not."'

On those occasions, as now, when Jessica attended a service, she felt a little like an actor on the wrong side of the footlights, detached and inclined to be cynical. It was she who had dusted the altar, polished the lectern, swept and hoovered, cleaned and tidied. It was she who, when the Eucharist was to be celebrated, prepared the elements. But, by one of those curious psychological quirks, she retained an almost superstitious regard for the statue of Christ which dominated the approach to the chancel. The statue was a loose 3-D rendering of Holman Hunt's excruciating painting, *The Light of the World*, differing mainly in that the statue held the lantern aloft.

Jessica always dusted the Christ figure with a feather duster, never allowing contact with her hands or her clothing and, in doing so, she avoided the eyes.

Now, while the vicar developed his theme, she found herself gazing at those eyes, though she could not see them distinctly, and she was disturbed; they seemed to be accusing, and she was filled with a sense of guilt.

'Now to God the Father, God the Son, and God the Holy Ghost . . .' A final hymn, the benediction, and the service drew to its end. With the church clock striking eleven the congregation trooped out into the sunshine.

Kathy said: 'Will you be in for lunch?'

Abe glanced at his watch. 'Christ, no! I've got a site meeting in St Austell and I'm late already.'

'It's Good Friday.'

'So what? It's easier without a lot of blokes around pretending to work. I'll collect the car and be off.'

Julie was hanging back. 'Aren't you coming home, kid?'

'I want a word with Giles.'

Geach muttered, 'That young wimp! She's hooked on him.'

Kathy turned to her sister. 'Why not stay and take pot luck with us, Jess?'

Jessica looked across to the porch where Stephanie Vinter was the centre of a congratulatory group, while her husband and son waited on the fringe. 'Thanks all the same, Kath, but it doesn't look as though anybody else intends to do any work this morning, so I'd better.'

She set off up Church Lane.

The Vinters got away at last and started walking up the

hill. Giles saw Julie waiting and joined her; his parents walked on.

Stephanie said, 'Are you ill, Laurence?'

'No.'

'There's something the matter with you.'

'Doesn't that apply to each of us?'

'Don't fence. You're cutting yourself off. Sometimes I wonder if . . .'

'What do you wonder?'

'Nothing. Here's Giles. What did Julie want?'

'She wanted me to go out with her this afternoon.'

'Are you going?'

'No.'

'What's the matter between you and Julie?'

'Nothing.'

Easter Saturday

On Saturday evening Jessica went as usual to do one of her stints at the church. She entered by the south door in her stockinged feet, having kicked off her half-wellies in the porch. No point in getting river mud on the nice carpet; she would only have to clean it up. It was overcast and raining and, though it was light enough outside, inside the light was dim; the lantern held aloft by the Christ figure glowed like a maleficent eye and she looked away. The altar and chancel were barely visible in the gloom.

Following an unconscious routine, she dropped the padlock on a little table next to the visitors' book and walked down the carpeted aisle. The chancel tiles were cold to her feet. After the severities of Lent there were flowers everywhere – lilies and tulips, ready for Sunday – Easter Sunday. The flower ladies had been and there would be a mess in the vestry toilet where they got their water.

Cleaning up messes was work for the peasantry.

She was on her way to the vestry; the self-closing door from the chancel was wedged open – the ladies again. She tried to shut it but it wouldn't budge. In the vestry she removed her mac and hood, and put on an old pair of slippers which she kept in a cupboard with her cleaning gear.

First things first: the Lenten hangings which had been in place through Passion-tide had been taken down but they must be brushed and folded away with their mothballs.

Jessica worked with seemingly effortless ease, but her thoughts were elsewhere; she was thinking of her sister. Kathy has everything a woman could want; she doesn't have to do a hand's turn if she doesn't want to. And if she took the trouble to understand him, she could twist Abe around her little finger.

While I . . . What do I do? I work like a slave for little more than subsistence, and I play the whore for nothing. Yet we are twins, two peas from the same pod. Why do I do it? To stop myself thinking? . . . As a punishment? . . . And what about him? Does he have nights when he forces himself to lie awake for fear of nightmares? . . . Always the same: the boy's white face, and his eyes staring up through the spokes of the cycle wheel. As I move away, those eyes seem to follow me . . .

She had brushed and folded away the hangings; now she was dealing with the vestry door. The flower arrangers had forced the wooden wedge in too far and she couldn't shift it. A hammer: there were a few tools in a cupboard in the tower, a hammer amongst them. She went to fetch it and while she was there the church clock went through its groans, grunts and clatter, preparatory to striking seven. She found the hammer and returned with it to the wedged door. Stooping, she swung it very gently, nudging the wedge.

'Practising your croquet, Jessica, or is it golf?'

She was startled. It was Arnold Paul, the organist, for whom she now worked a couple of afternoons a week. Plump, amiable, and a trifle smug, he was standing in the aisle, watching her.

'It's jammed. One of the women on flowers this week doesn't know her own strength.'

'I came in to collect some music.' He crossed to the organ console and was hidden by the curtain.

The wedge was freed and the door to the vestry closed. The organ played softly, an odd little tune. Jessica had no ear for music. Next on her schedule: cleaning the vestry toilet. The floor was swimming with water mixed with leaves, flower stalks, and wrapping tissue; five or six unwanted vases had not been put away.

When she returned to the church the organ was silent and there was no sign of Arnold. Odd. He usually called out when he was going. Perhaps he had. She crossed to the console, there was no-one there and the lid was down over the keys. She was being foolish, yet she was tempted to wedge the south door shut. But that would be too absurd.

Saturday evening routine dictated two more jobs: a whisk round with a feather duster on the altar and chancel, and a bit of elbow grease on the lectern to bring up the shine. It was while she was dusting that she thought she heard a movement somewhere in the body of the church.

'Is anyone there?'

She was unusually nervous. Why am I so jumpy? She followed the same routine in the depth of winter on nights when, without a torch, it would have been impossible to find her way through the churchyard. She called again with no reply and she went on with her work. Then there was someone – the vicar. She was polishing the lectern.

'Good evening, Jessica. I hope I didn't startle you? I came across to fetch my nice new service book.'

She was glad he had come.

Apart from anything else she liked the vicar, and it was not given to many to be liked by Jessica. She believed that he was a good man, and innocent; the sort who could touch filth without being soiled, perhaps without even knowing.

'I'm almost through.'

'It all looks splendid, Jessica, but then, it always does. I really don't know what we would do without you.'

Easter Sunday

The following morning at seven-fifteen, Michael Jordan, Vicar of Moresk, crossed the road from the vicarage to his church. At thirty-eight, he was unmarried, and his sister, Celia, several years older, kept house for him. It was a balmy spring morning but whatever the weather, in winter darkness or in the brash light of high summer, he took pleasure in so beginning his day. He felt part of the great Christian tradition which, probably on this very site, reached back to the missionary work of St Sulien, patron saint of his church, among the heathen Celts.

He passed through the sixteenth-century lich-gate, followed the gravelled walk among the gravestones, glimpsed the river between the trees, and arrived at the south porch. To his astonishment he heard the sound of the organ, a sustained chord of discordant notes. He had in his hand the key to a padlock by which the church was supposedly secured against latter-day Vandals but the padlock was missing and the heavy oaken door with its wrought-iron latch and ring stood open.

He experienced a tremor of disquiet; an awareness, as he interpreted it, of the proximity of Evil. Michael saw himself and the rest of mankind doing daily battle with

Evil which, for him, was a positive and potent force. He pushed the door wide and was somewhat reassured to see the padlock on the table just inside the door, next to the visitors' book and offertory box. But the vibrant dissonance of the organ chord filled the church, setting his teeth and his nerves on edge. He looked across at the console but the curtain hid anyone who might have been there. Somebody playing the fool?

He entered the nave, genuflected towards the altar and, in the act, caught sight of a figure sprawled across the chancel steps. His fears intensified. Summoning his courage he walked down the aisle and approached the steps. Jessica Dobell lay on her back, diagonally across the steps, and she was certainly dead. Her head was turned slightly to the right and her skull had been smashed, just forward of the crown. Her hair around the injury was a mass of clotted blood, while something more viscous than blood had oozed on to the tiled step. Her blue denim shirt had been ripped open, exposing her breasts; and her jeans, unzipped, had been dragged part-way down her thighs along with her briefs.

Adding to his horror and sense of desecration, she was lying at the very feet of the statue of Christ; Christ with his lantern held aloft – *Lux Mundi* – *The Light of the World*.

Jessica's hair was spread out so that it reached, and partly covered, the bare feet of the statue, and Michael was irresistibly reminded of Mary Magdalene who anointed the feet of Jesus with her perfume and 'wiped them with her hair till the house was filled with the fragrance'. Always a little disturbed by the image which that passage conjured up, he was deeply distressed that his mind should seize upon it at such a moment. Instinctively he crossed himself and murmured an incoherent prayer.

Only last night . . . Had she been there ever since?

Although he was filled with revulsion he could not keep

his eyes from her body. He was astonished to see that, away from her injury, her features were composed; she looked in death as she had been in life, a very attractive woman. If only her breasts and thighs were covered . . . He stooped, with the foolish intention of drawing her shirt-front together, but stopped himself in time. The police would take a poor view of such interference and there was no possible doubt that they must be involved.

The continuing, droning chord on the organ made it impossible to think. He could hear the muffled purr of the electric blower and, as he approached the console, he saw that five notes, apparently chosen at random in the 'great', were permanently depressed by little wedges of paper, folded to the appropriate thickness and inserted between the keys. Once more he was on the point of committing a blunder – by removing the wedges; instead, he switched off the blower and silence descended like a benediction.

What he had to do was clear: he must lock the church, go back to the vicarage and telephone the police. But he really could not persuade himself to leave the poor woman so obscenely exposed. He went to the vestry and returned with a surplice which, with great gentleness, he arranged to his satisfaction.

Then he prayed briefly, genuflected, and left.

Eight o'clock Holy Communion was celebrated at St Sulien's each Sunday but, on this special Sunday which commemorated the risen Lord, those who came would find their church locked against them.

Forty odd miles away, as crows are said to fly, on the estuary of the Tamar, Detective Chief Superintendent Charles Wycliffe was in his garden accompanied by the cat, Macavity. The pond had recently been cleaned and refurbished so that now, its ecological equanimity disturbed, it had produced inordinate quantities of blanket weed. Wycliffe, armed with a trident-like weapon, had lifted out a mass of the green, filamentous, slimy stuff and from it he now rescued trapped newts, tadpoles, young frogs, and nymphs of dragonflies, all to be returned to the pond.

But not snails. Helen was adamant. There were too many snails, so those that were found must be banished into the outer darkness. He disliked such a god-like decisive role but the task was otherwise agreeable; contemplative, and on balance constructive, ideally suited to his middle-aged psyche.

Macavity, more virile in his pursuits and aspirations, put on his mouse-hunting act. Watching some phantom rodent, whiskers a-tremble and tail rigid, he would stalk the imagined quarry and, insinuating his plump body through the herbage with infinite care, the mighty hunter would crouch, ready for the spring – then pounce.

All this despite the fact that the sight of a can of Whiskas, preferably open, was necessary to induce in Macavity any sign of a salivary reflex.

The Wycliffes would never see fifty again; they were on the slope – definitely. For twenty years they had lived in the Watch House, a former coastguard station converted to a dwelling house, and their half-acre of garden sloped to the narrows where the estuary met the sea. Were they happy? Wycliffe told himself that happiness is a peak experience that comes in small doses – a few seconds at a time; at most a few hours. But they were content; content with each other and with their lot.

After rearing their two children they were mostly alone again. The boy, David, was married and more or less settled in Kenya with his wife and child; while their daughter, Ruth, lived with her former boss in a nebulous relationship so far unproductive of offspring.

Easter Sunday: the church bells of St Juliot, their nearest village, were pealing in celebration and their sound rose and fell, carried on a fitful breeze. The air was soft and warm. Wycliffe knew that it was going to be one of those idyllic days, always to be remembered. For a few hours at least the Watch House and its garden would become an exclusion zone within which he, Helen, and Macavity would pursue their separate illusions in blissful relaxation.

He was wrong.

Helen's voice came from the terrace. 'Telephone!' And, as he reached her, she said, 'It's Lucy Lane.'

Detective Sergeant Lucy Lane was the day's duty officer in CID. 'Sorry to disturb your Sunday, sir, but there's a report from C Division, logged at 09.33. At about 07.30 this morning, Jessica Dobell, a woman in her late thirties, was found dead in St Sulien's Church, in the village of Moresk, near Truro. She appears to have died from a depressed fracture of the skull caused by a powerful blow. DI Rowse from sub-division, attending, says it's murder.'

'You did say Moresk?'

'I did, sir.'

'That's only a few miles from the Duloe place.'*

'A bit nearer Truro, and on the other side of the river.'

'What on earth's happening down there?'

'I've no idea, sir; perhaps they get bored in the off season.' Lucy Lane had little time for rhetorical questions.

Wycliffe sighed as he replaced the telephone. A well established routine made detailed instructions unnecessary. DI Kersey, on call, would gather together a small headquarters team while the local inspector would call in the police surgeon, inform relatives, arrange formal

**Wycliffe and the Dead Flautist*

identification, and notify the coroner. But Wycliffe must visit the scene and, according to what he saw and heard, decide whether or not to become personally involved.

'A murder, apparently, at Moresk, near Truro.'

'I'll make some coffee.'

Helen was by no means indifferent to tragedy but when crime and violence are woven into the fabric of daily life an extra skin is part of the survival kit.

'Are you likely to be home this evening?'

'Possibly, it's only fifty-odd miles.'

Helen grinned. 'Some of them very odd, as I remember. Anyhow, I'll put your weekend bag in the car. Go and make yourself respectable.'

So much for his Easter Sunday.

Helen was right; getting on to the spine road from the complex of creeks and streams which is the Tamar valley, and off it, to that not dissimilar complex which is the valley of the Fal, makes an interesting experience. Wycliffe was not a good driver; in fact he had no rapport with any mechanical device more complex than a can opener, and the journey took him longer than it should have done. 'Turn off left in Tresillian', he told himself. He did, then got lost in a bewildering maze of lanes, narrow and tortuous, and peopled by stolid men in large cars who simply stopped and waited with patronizing patience for him to extricate himself from every impasse.

He finally arrived in the village as the church clock was striking twelve.

Chapter Two

Easter Sunday (continued)

Moresk village and a patch of woodland on the other side of Truro are almost all that survive to perpetuate the name of that great forest of Morrois where Tristan fled with Iseult, only to be discovered by King Mark. Although the village is quite close to Truro it was Wycliffe's first visit, and he was surprised to find such a populous little place tucked away in one of the creeks. He stopped in the square which, on one side, was bounded by the foreshore and the waters of the creek. Small boats were stranded on the shingle, lying at odd angles, and a pair of swans waddled around the garage forecourt among the petrol pumps. He decided at once that he liked the place.

He could see the church through trees away to his left but separated from the square by a substantial house in its own grounds. He left his car, found Church Lane, and a minute or two later arrived at the lich-gate where a small crowd had gathered under the eye of a uniformed policeman.

'DI Reed is in the church, sir.'

Wycliffe found the south porch and entered the church. Coming in out of the sunlight, the nave seemed to be in near darkness though the chancel and altar were floodlit like a stage set. Three men were in conversation near the chancel steps and one of them came to greet him. It was DI Reed.

Reed and Wycliffe had worked together several times. He was a large man with a high colour, fleshy features, and a neck which bulged over his collar. A fringe of red hair surrounded a bald patch. 'Welcome aboard, sir.'

Reed led him to the chancel steps. Tread boards were in place to protect whatever evidence there might be until scenes-of-crime had finished. The body was sprawled across the steps, at the very feet of a statue of Christ. The head to one side exposed a ghastly wound to the parietal region of the skull.

Wycliffe stood gazing down at this woman whose concerns in life had now, by reason of her death, become his. What shocked him most about violent death was the ease with which the thread is snapped; but here was something more, something bizarre, and he was troubled.

'She wasn't killed here, like that – the body has been arranged.' A banal observation but something was expected of him and it was all he could find to say.

Reed, at ease, comfortable, said, 'No, she was dragged from over by the pulpit. There's blood on the tiles there, and traces in between.'

Wycliffe could scarcely take his eyes from the body. Never before had he been confronted with a murder which made such a profound first impression; yet he found difficulty in putting that impression into words.

Ripping open the victim's blouse to expose the breasts is a common enough feature of sexual assault on a woman, but jeans and briefs had been pulled down just far enough to uncover the pubic triangle – and no further. Her body had been arranged in an abandoned pose across the chancel steps and her abundant hair, dark and lustrous, had been ordered so that it reached and spread over the sandalled feet of Christ.

What he was seeing was a set piece such as a surrealist sculptor might devise in order to shock, and so to make a point. But to prepare this set piece and make whatever point was intended, a woman had been murdered.

Belatedly he noticed that she was wearing bedroom slippers, an old pair that had seen better days.

Reed said, 'That's how she was found, sir; nothing has been disturbed except that a surplice, used by the vicar to cover her, was taken away. No sign of any footwear other than those slippers, and she didn't walk here in those.'

'Doesn't it strike you as . . . as grotesque?'

Reed puffed out his cheeks. 'Kinky is the word that comes to mind. If it was a sexual assault it didn't achieve a climax.' Reed smoothed his bald patch with an enormous, freckled paw. 'My guess is that it was never intended to, but what was intended, God only knows.'

'What was she doing in the church?'

'She was a sort of caretaker-cum-verger and she looked in on Saturday evenings to make sure everything was ready for Sunday.'

'Next of kin?'

'There's only a sister and she's been told. Deceased wasn't married. There's a smallholding just up-river from here which she ran with the help of a couple living in. They've been notified. The sister lives in Trigg House, adjoining the churchyard, and she's married to Abe Geach, the contractor.' A quick look. 'Does that mean anything to you, sir?'

'Should it?'

Reed shrugged. 'Money. He's got contracts all over the two counties and he's one of those who manages to keep warm and dry whatever the financial climate. I mention it because he carries quite a bit of weight around here.'

'She has no parents living?'

'Both killed in a coach crash several years back.'

DS Fox, Wycliffe's scenes-of-crime officer, had completed his first series of photographs of the body but more would be taken when the pathologist arrived and it could be disturbed. Now Fox turned his attention to the immediate setting.

Wycliffe, as always, was fascinated by Fox; it was an experience to see him go to work. He would arrive, unburdened, followed by his assistant, the long-suffering Collis, laden like a Spaniard's donkey. A room, a river bank, an alley, a night-club, or a church, it was all the same to Fox. He seemed to show not the slightest interest in his surroundings in general but concentrated on each item or aspect as it presented itself to him on some mental list. A wizard with molehills, he was apt to miss the occasional mountain.

Brooding, Wycliffe turned once more to the inspector. 'The weapon?'

Reed pointed. Lying at some distance from the body, near the pulpit, and barely visible in its shadow, was a long-handled hammer with a smallish head. 'It's an unusual sort, sir – like they used to use for wheel-tapping on the railway.'

Stooping, Wycliffe could see that the head was encrusted with dried blood and there was blood on the tiles.

Wycliffe returned to the chancel steps and the body. 'Presumably she's been here all night. What was the weather like yesterday evening?'

'Wet. It rained all the evening, sir; I checked.'

'So it's unlikely that she came here dressed like this.'

'She didn't; there's a heavy mac with a hood in the vestry but, as I said, no footwear. I understand she usually came to work along the river bank and that must have been pretty muddy. What she wore on her feet is a bit of a puzzle at the moment.'

Wycliffe was soaking up all the detail of which he was capable. His questions were curt and there were intervals during which he stood, staring down at the dead woman or watching Fox's antics with the camera.

'Who found her?'

'The vicar: the Reverend Michael Jordan. There he is . . .' Reed indicated a youngish man in clerical garb, seated in one of the pews, head bent, eyes closed, as though in prayer.

Now that Wycliffe had become accustomed to the uneven lighting he could see that the church must have the support of dedicated and well-heeled parishioners. There was an impressive tapestry above the altar and the altar cloth was elaborately embroidered; the aisles and the pews were carpeted and many of the pews sported embroidered hassocks on which the knees of the devout might rest at ease. Flowers were everywhere and the air was heavy with their scent, blending with the lingering tangy odour of incense.

'What did the doctor have to say?'

'He's still here. That's him, talking to my sergeant – Dr Sparrow. I think he's loath to go; he's not often in the limelight and I suppose it's a change from sore throats and backaches.'

The doctor was in his early sixties, short, stocky and weather-beaten. Dressed in shabby tweeds he was almost a caricature of the traditional country doctor.

'You don't need me to tell you what she died of but you might want my view on when. My guess would be, sometime last evening, between eight or nine and midnight. I can't do better than that but I imagine you will have Franks to do the clever stuff.'

'And the sexual aspect?'

The doctor pouted. 'What about it? The chap obviously didn't really get around to it. I imagine the situation was a bit off-putting.'

'One more question, Dr Sparrow – not a professional one – are you acquainted with the vicar?'

'I know him, naturally, but I'm no churchgoer.'

'An unbiased view, then. What sort of man is he?'

Sparrow chuckled. 'So that's how you blokes go about it! Well, I'd say he was a sincere, hardworking chap; always on call – like me.' A sly grin.

'Popular?'

'I think so; he's pushed up church attendance, so they tell me, and despite his Holy-Joe appearance and manner, he's accepted by the young. They call him Michael, or even Mike. He didn't go down well with the diehards at first, but they seem to have come round. Why don't you have a chat with him?'

'I'm going to.' Wycliffe thanked the doctor.

Jordan got up from his seat as Wycliffe approached. His blond hair clipped short and his smooth, pink, unblemished skin gave him an unused look, reminiscent of a young baby. Wycliffe had the uncomfortable feeling that he might be dealing with a postulant for sainthood.

The preliminaries over, Jordan said, 'This morning I was due to celebrate Holy Communion at eight, and matins at eleven . . . Now, I suppose, it will be some time before I can conduct any services here at all . . . Apart from anything else there is the question of desecration. The bishop will have to decide what is to be done . . .' The blue eyes were troubled.

'How long have you been in Moresk, Vicar?'

'Four years at Michaelmas.'

'So you must know the people. This woman, Jessica Dobell . . . I understand she kept the church clean.'

'That is an understatement; Jessica saw to everything, from cleaning, to preparations for the different services. I don't know what we shall do without her.'

'You've seen the weapon?'

The vicar nodded. 'It comes from a cupboard in the tower where we keep all sorts of things which might be handy about the church – from flower vases to drawing pins. It's horrible to think . . .'

'I gather that the dead woman didn't live with any relative.'

'No, Jessica had certain views about marriage and family life . . .' His eyes sought Wycliffe's and seemed to beg for understanding. 'You will hear rumours . . . gossip.'

Reed and the vicar between them were opening up vistas, giving Wycliffe his first glimpse of the people whose intimate lives would be his concern in the days or weeks ahead. It was his job to invite their confidence and probe their deceptions until a rather special kind of truth was established – that arcane variety which is recognized in the Courts.

As always, he felt a stirring of excitement at the prospect; an excitement tinged with the guilt of a voyeur.

'If I might suggest, Mr Wycliffe . . .' The vicar was nervous but resolved to make his point. 'If I might suggest, it could be a mistake to approach this young woman with a prejudice. After all, a certain laxness in sexual matters does not necessarily mean that those concerned are not caring and hard-working people.'

Verily, a saint! But Wycliffe was mildly snubbing. 'I try not to prejudge anybody, Mr Jordan.

'Now, you must have noticed that the dead woman is wearing slippers—'

The vicar smiled. 'Jessica always wore slippers when she was working, and always the same old pair. She kept them in a cupboard in the vestry. You see, she walked to work by way of the river bank, which is always muddy, wearing short wellingtons which she left in the porch.'

'Show me.'

He was conducted to the south porch with its slatted seats and notice boards but there were no boots.

Jordan was puzzled. 'That is strange.'

Back in the church Wycliffe said, 'One more question, Mr Jordan, and I want you to think carefully before you answer. Apart from the south door being unlocked and the body on the chancel steps, was there anything else, however trivial, which struck you as unusual when you arrived this morning?'

The vicar put his hand to his forehead. 'Of course! The organ! It's hard to believe, but that went entirely from my mind . . . Anyway, I'll show you.'

Wycliffe followed him to the organ console.

'An instrument of this quality – it's a two-manual Willis – may strike you as a little out of place in a country church like ours, but Arnold Paul, our unpaid organist, rescued it from a disused London church, had it dismantled, renovated, and rebuilt here – all at his own expense.'

'What about it?'

'Yes, of course! I digress. If I switch on the blower you will understand.'

The vicar threw a switch and the church was once more filled with a nagging discordance.

'You see that certain notes in the "great" are wedged down with folded bits of paper and when I arrived this morning this rather distressing sound greeted me along with the rest.'

'Does it mean anything to you?'

The vicar looked blank. 'Nothing at all!'

'Anyway, switch it off.' Wycliffe waited until peace was restored, then: 'This organist . . .'

'Mr Arnold Paul – he lives almost opposite the church; a man of independent means, a keen and able musician. I would have expected him to be here but he was probably prevented by your man at the gate.'

'I'll send for him. Just one more question, Mr Jordan.

Would you have expected to find Jessica here when you arrived this morning?'

'Oh, no. She was only concerned with the preparations, not with the actual services.'

'And yesterday evening?'

'Yes, she usually comes – came in on Saturday evenings. She liked to have everything spick and span for Sunday.'

Crossing over by the chancel steps Wycliffe asked Fox, 'Anything to tell me? What about the weapon – any prints?'

'The weapon has been wiped clean; in fact there are no significant prints anywhere that I've examined so far.'

'All right. When you've finished here, take a look at the organ console – you'll see why when you get there. I shall want photographs. Pay special attention to the paper or card used to wedge the keys but don't disturb anything until the organist has seen it.'

He left the church and walked in the churchyard. Unlike Fox, he felt a compelling need to fit the crime and the scene of the crime into a broader context.

The church was built on sloping ground between the creek and the river; a fringe of pines and a scattering of ash and lime trees offered shelter in winter and shade in summer. Through the trees he could see the grey roofs of a substantial old house, presumably Trigg, where the dead woman's sister lived with her affluent husband. Beyond the house he glimpsed the silvery waters of the creek.

The earliest tombstones he could find dated from the sixteen-nineties and there were not many later than the nineteen-sixties when, with the dead making increasing demands on the land of the living, cremation became necessary as well as fashionable. He was interested in the names: Angove, Geach, Carveth, Noall, Dobell . . .

One of the newer stones caught his eye: 'In loving memory of our dear parents, John and Katherine Dobell, killed in a coach accident, 23rd September 1975. This stone is erected by their twin daughters: Katherine and Jessica.'

The churchyard was well but not obsessively cared for so that primroses flourished and bluebells were sprouting.

'Nice place!'

It was Doug Kersey, his principal assistant and colleague for twenty years.

'So you've arrived.'

'I brought Shaw and Potter; Lucy Lane is following on with Dixon.'

'Have you been inside?'

'I had a look and a word with Reed. What is it? Some sort of ritual killing – or what?'

'Or what, I should think.'

'It's bloody queer, anyway.'

A relief not to have to spell everything out.

'There's a guy in there, says he's the organist and that you want to speak to him.'

'Have you heard anything of Franks?' Franks was the pathologist.

'They couldn't find him at first but they've run him to earth. He's down here, spending Easter with friends in St Mawes. He should be along at any minute but he won't be pleased, that's for sure.'

It would have been easy to write Kersey off as a hard-faced cop. He looked the part and, to some extent, it was the image he cultivated. But, early in their association, Wycliffe had discovered behind the mask a moral and compassionate man.

Wycliffe found the organist sitting in a pew at the back of the church. As it happened, the sun was striking down through a stained-glass window in the south wall suffusing the man's face with a rosy pink glow. Paul was in his late fifties but his hair was white; he was plump, smooth-skinned, meticulously groomed, and soberly dressed. Wycliffe recalled Mr Polly's 'portly capon' and smiled secretly.

Wycliffe held out his hand. 'Mr Paul? Have they shown you your organ?'

'I've been shown nothing. I was told to sit here and wait.'

Evidently a man not accustomed to being instructed, but he was not slow to thaw. He stood, looking down at the wedged keys. 'How very odd!'

'Do you make anything of it?'

Paul fingered his smooth chin. 'I hesitate to answer that because the notion seems so utterly absurd. On the other hand, those notes could hardly have been chosen by chance.'

'Tell me.'

'Doesn't that combination mean anything to you?'

'I'm afraid not.'

'Well, the depressed notes are A,B,E,G, and a second G, an octave higher: the notes used by Schumann in his Variations to flatter Meta von Abegg, his girlfriend of that time.'

Wycliffe, despite Helen's efforts, knew little about music but he thought he knew the keyboard. He said, with diffidence, 'But isn't the second note, the black one, B flat?'

The organist was impatient. 'Of course it is, in our notation; but the Germans call it B, which is what Schumann did. That fact, if nothing else, makes it certain that these notes were not chosen at random.'

'Can you suggest any reason why someone might want to draw attention to this piece of music in such dramatic circumstances?'

Paul looked at him with puzzled eyes. 'It means nothing to me. I can't understand it.'

'The dead woman was employed to clean the church so, presumably, you knew her?'

The abrupt change of subject was too much for Paul's precisely ordered mind but he made the effort. 'Knew her? Of course I knew her; and not only through her work here. A few weeks ago I persuaded her to work for me part-time in the house. She came two days a week – Tuesdays and Fridays – for three hours each afternoon. She was very good and, surprisingly, she hit it off with my old housekeeper who is not the easiest of women to get along with.'

'Was she interested in music?'

'Not as far as I am aware.'

'Would you say that anyone setting up this charade needed to be knowledgeable about music?'

Paul hesitated. 'It depends what you mean by knowledgeable. I am sure that a great many people who would not think of themselves as particularly musical would know of the Abegg Variations and of the differences between our notation and the German.'

'Just one more question, Mr Paul – one that will be asked of everyone in any way involved – where were you between, say, seven-thirty and midnight last night?'

'I was at home.'

'Anyone to substantiate that?'

Paul hesitated. 'My housekeeper, I suppose, but she is very deaf and, as we were not in the same room, her evidence may not be reliable.'

There would be more questions for the organist but now Wycliffe wanted to broaden his approach, to get some idea of the probable scope of his inquiry. And Dr Franks had arrived.

Wycliffe joined the pathologist as he stood, taking in the disturbing spectacle of the obscenely exposed body of a murdered woman sprawled at the feet of a holy statue.

Franks was short, not really fat, but a roly-poly of a man. He was cynical, as most pathologists are, but good humoured, as many are not. More to the point, Wycliffe respected his judgement.

Franks said, 'I suppose you realize you've spoilt my holiday?'

'It's a habit I have. What do you make of it?'

Franks, unusually sombre, admitted, 'I thought I'd lost the capacity for surprise, Charles. On the face of it I shan't be much use to you; the forensic aspects seem plain enough. But my guess is you'll be up to your neck in trick cyclists if it ever comes to court. Anyway, let's get on. If Fox is ready to take his pictures . . .'

When Franks had made his preliminary examination, he said, 'Well, it all seems consistent with a nasty knock on the head and I shall be surprised if I have much more to tell you after the autopsy.'

'Nothing on the relative positions of attacker and attacked?'

Franks shrugged. 'If you think it would help, I don't mind doing your job for you. The cranium was fractured in the region of the left parietal, not far from the sagittal suture – in other words, near the top of the head. My guess is that she was stooping or crouching at the time, that her attacker was to her left, and that she raised her head to look up at him as the blow fell. How's that?'

'The power behind the blow?'

Pause for thought. 'The long handle, with a good swing, would generate plenty of momentum without much muscle power behind it. The hammer head isn't very heavy but it didn't need to be.'

'So it could have been a man or a woman?'

Franks nodded. 'Yes, sex doesn't enter the picture from that angle but there seems to be plenty of it about otherwise.'

'Time of death?'

A chubby grimace. 'She seems to have been what the books call "a sound muscular subject" and she was doing moderately energetic things before she got clobbered. On the other hand the temperature in this place in the late evening and night can't be anything to write home about.' He was bending over the body once more, attempting to flex an arm. 'Now, as you see, rigor is on the way out . . . Taken with the body temperature . . .'

Wycliffe said, 'Well? Do I have to do my own sums?'

'I'd give it between seventeen and twenty hours. What is it now – about three? . . . Say between seven and ten last night. If I had to be more precise I'd go for mid-way between the two, but don't put much on that.'

Kathy was in the garden, standing by the steep bank which was almost a wall, the boundary separating Trigg from the churchyard. There were clumps of primroses and the hawthorn bushes which surmounted the bank were coming into leaf. Through the screen of twigs she could see the graves, and the church itself, mellow, lichen-encrusted stones which looked as old as time.

And Jessica was lying dead, just that little distance away. At some time during the evening or night Jessica, in some ways her yardstick, her touchstone, had been viciously murdered. She tried but failed to grasp what it would mean to her. The little policewoman in her trim uniform – a girl in her twenties – had tried to cover her feeling of inadequacy with a professional gloss. 'Your sister would have known almost nothing, Mrs Geach. The doctor says death was instantaneous.'

She had never imagined life without Jessica and she could not now. It was strange, for in recent years they had not been close. Not since . . . Since when? . . . Her marriage to Abe? No, their intimacy had survived that. It dated from Jessica's break with Johnny Glynn. Something to do with the death of the Ruse boy? That seemed to be what Jess was hinting at on Wednesday at the farm. She had been on the point of confiding something, but had changed her mind. At any rate it was sixteen years since they had ceased being twins and had become merely sisters.

Now Katherine felt that she wanted to weep for Jessica, for herself, and for the might-have-been.

'I think you should come indoors; it's clouding over and getting chilly out here.' Abe had arrived, ponderously solicitous.

'I'm not cold.'

'Vinter has been on the phone.'

'What does he want?'

'Well, it's only natural he should want to make contact.'

She was venomous. 'All they're worrying about is being kicked out of the farm, but they've got some explaining to do.'

'Explaining? You don't think they had anything to do with it?'

'Why wasn't I told – why wasn't anybody told – that Jess didn't come home last night? It was the police who went to them, not the other way round.'

He put his arm around her. 'Come in and have a hot drink – a toddy is the thing for you, my girl!'

For some reason Katherine was incensed by his attention and broke away. 'Lay off, Abe, for God's sake! You think everything can be cured by sex or alcohol – or both.'

Chapter Three

Easter Sunday afternoon

The headquarters team mustered by Kersey had arrived: Detective Sergeants Lucy Lane and Shaw; and Detective Constables Dixon and Potter – known, because of their respective physiques, as Pole and Pot. With help from the local police, Sergeant Shaw, the squad's Pooh-Bah, wearing his administrative hat, was involved in arranging accommodation for the team and finding a hall or other building which could be used as an Incident Room. The two DCs, again with local support, would be concerned with interviews and inquiries under Kersey's direction.

All of which left Wycliffe free to assume his preferred role, a roving commission, getting to know everybody who was, or might be, involved – in particular, the victim. He considered whether to begin with the sister and brother-in-law at Trigg, but decided on the farm because that was where the victim had lived her life.

He conscripted Lucy Lane – Detective Sergeant Lucy Lane, in her thirties, dark, warm-skinned and eligible, but still single. 'I wouldn't inflict this world on a child of mine. I see too much of it.'

A sentiment which shocked Wycliffe to whom hope was an ultimate resource.

'Shall I get the car?'

'No, let's walk.'

It was characteristic that he should walk rather than

drive or be driven; he refused to allow his days to become crowded with events in a frenetic succession of images like a television screen, lacking even commercial breaks to aid digestion.

The immediate countryside about Moresk is one of low, rounded hills and gentle slopes, moist lanes and trickling water. Standing by the ramshackle gate which led to the farm they could follow the course of the river as it narrowed and was lost between the slopes. No more than a quarter of a mile away a rambling old house in a hotch-potch of styles, not unlike Trigg but larger, fronted on the river. It was backed by a plantation of larches and, on the rising ground behind, a tower dominated the Lilliputian landscape.

Wycliffe said, 'What is it? It looks like a lighthouse.'

It had the proportions of a factory chimney, but it had lancet windows and, at the top, a domed structure slightly greater in diameter than the tower.

Lucy, who had relatives in the county and knew about such things, said, 'I suppose it's a folly. Anyway, it belongs to the Carey family who live in the big house – what's left of them – and it.'

Wycliffe had a weakness for follies and promised himself closer acquaintance with the tower but he had no intimation then of the circumstances which would bring this about.

They passed through the farm gate, and between tethered goats, down the slope to the farmyard which vividly recalled Wycliffe's own childhood. In the yard a man in bib-and-brace overalls was scattering handfuls of grain for the chickens. It was like being in a time warp of fifty years.

'Mr Vinter?'

The man was very tall; thin, and bony, with that stoop which is sometimes habitual to the tall. He seemed to study Wycliffe for a while before speaking, his blue eyes expressionless, then, 'Laurence Vinter – yes. Are you a policeman?'

'Chief Superintendent Wycliffe. This is Detective Sergeant Lane.'

'You'd better come inside.'

They were taken into the sitting room where a woman sat by the window, reading. The light from the window with its tiny panes fell on one side of her face and form, leaving the rest in shadow. She was very fair, with an oval face and perfect features; her straight hair, with its meticulous central parting, precisely framed her face and was caught up in a coil at the back. She wore a blue pinafore frock over a print blouse.

'My wife, Stephanie; Chief Superintendent Wycliffe . . . Detective Sergeant Lane.'

Stephanie Vinter rested her book, still open, on the windowsill, and stood up, eyeing the policewoman. Her little blue eyes were hard.

On the face of it the Vinters were an oddly assorted couple, the woman, small, refined – exquisite; the man, ungainly, angular, and somehow unfinished. But they shared a certain deliberation in speech and manner as though they existed in a world where the pace of life was slower.

The preliminaries over, Wycliffe was seated in a wicker chair which creaked, while Lucy was given a hard kitchen chair which did not. Wycliffe began his questions. 'When did you last see Miss Dobell?'

The two looked at each other and, after a pause, it was the woman who answered, 'Last evening, at about seven. We have our meal at six . . .'

Laurence Vinter said, 'She always goes to the church on Saturday evening to make sure that everything is right for Sunday.'

'But last evening she didn't come back.'

'No.'

Wycliffe was impatient. 'Didn't you expect her back? Weren't you concerned?'

It seemed for a moment that they had no more to say, then Laurence spoke: 'You must understand that our position here is somewhat equivocal. I mean we are not family; we live here in return for helping out on the farm.'

It was Lucy's turn. 'But surely that doesn't mean that you were indifferent to her being out all night with no news?'

Another silence. Laurence Vinter studied his long bony fingers, his wife looked across at him, her gaze expressionless. Wycliffe would have liked to shake them both. 'Well?'

Finally Laurence raised his head. 'It wasn't unusual for Jessica to be away all night.'

'Without warning you?'

'Yes.'

'Have you any idea where she spent those nights?'

'No, and she wouldn't have welcomed any question or comment.'

'How often did this happen?'

Laurence shrugged. 'Three or four times a month? Probably about that.'

'Was it always a Saturday night?' From Lucy Lane.

'On the contrary, it was usually mid-week.'

'Was she ever away for more than one night?'

'A couple of times but then she warned us in advance.'

Wycliffe turned to the woman. 'Presumably, if she intended to be away, she took an overnight bag or something . . .'

'No. She left here the same, whatever her intentions, dressed for the weather as it happened to be.'

'She had a car?'

'No, there is a truck, but that is used only for farm work.'

'So she left here yesterday evening, just after seven, to walk to the church. Is that right?'

'After our meal, as my wife said. It was raining, and she put on her heavy mac with a hood, and the short wellingtons she wears about the farm.'

A collie dog padded into the room, looked and sniffed around, then went out disconsolate.

Wycliffe said, 'How long have you lived with Miss Dobell?'

'Three years last month.'

'Before that?'

Vinter, after the customary pause, said, 'I was a lecturer at Bristol; I had a breakdown and had to give it up.' He spoke slowly, as though his words were being dredged up from some deeper layer of consciousness. 'In the process we lost our home and it happened that we spent the winter of eighty-seven in temporary accommodation near here – a winter let. At the start of the holiday season we had to get out, and Jessica offered us accommodation on condition that Stephanie took on the housework and I helped on the farm.'

'You have no outside source of income?'

Stephanie intervened. 'That sounds impertinent, Superintendent, but I suppose you are interested in our bona fides. We have nothing to hide. Laurence receives a small pension from his former employment and he does a certain amount of translation work for a publisher.'

Wycliffe, trying to decide what it was about the woman that impressed him, concluded that above all else it was her serenity; everything about her was calm and cool and he wondered what it might take to ruffle the surface of her composure or raise her emotional temperature to blood heat.

Vinter found it necessary to supplement what his wife had said: 'I was a lecturer and tutor in modern languages, that is why I am able to undertake translation work. We get a small weekly payment and, of course, our living is free.'

It was Lucy who asked, 'What is likely to happen now?'

Vinter replied with a lift of the shoulders.

Wycliffe was looking across at a roll-top desk. 'Is that where Miss Dobell did her accounts?'

'Yes.'

'Miss Lane will go through its contents and I would like one of you to be with her.'

Once more the exchange of glances and Vinter stood up.

Wycliffe said, 'Where do you do your translation work, Mr Vinter?'

Vinter seemed surprised by the question. 'Upstairs; in our room.'

'May I see upstairs? Perhaps while Mr Vinter is occupied here . . . ?'

Stephanie said, 'If you wish.'

As he followed her up the crooked stairs he heard Vinter say, 'Jessica kept her desk locked, but the key is on a little hook in the knee-hole.'

On the landing, at the top of the stairs, three doors opened off. Stephanie pushed open all three. 'Jessica's is the double room at the front, ours is the double room at the back, and my son, Giles, has the box room.'

Both the larger rooms must have been furnished early in the century: the beds had brass rails with elaborate knobs, and in each there was a washstand with a flowered ewer and basin as well as a dressing table, a chest of drawers, and a wardrobe. The Vinters had an additional table – placed tight against the window; it held a few books and a portable typewriter, but books were also stacked against the walls on makeshift shelves and even piled on the floor. A tiny electric fire had its place near the table.

'This is where Laurence works.'

Jessica's room was characterless. Wycliffe opened the wardrobe and pulled out one or two drawers of the chest. The chest was full of bedding, and the clothes in the wardrobe seemed hardly to cater for the minimal needs of ordinary occasions or, indeed, for the succession of seasons.

The box room had space only for a single divan bed and a chest of drawers. Rows of books were lined up on the chest and a violin case lay on the bed.

'Your son plays the violin?'

'I am teaching him.'

'You are a musician?'

A slight shrug.

'Was Jessica musical?'

'Not as far as I know.'

They were on their way back down the stairs. 'There is a bathroom adjoining the kitchen, if you wish to see it.'

She was being ironic but Wycliffe said, politely, 'Thank you.'

There was a great deal that he wanted to ask but very little that he would learn from her answers; he wanted gossip, and she was no gossip. Lucy was still busy at the desk, while Laurence stood by showing little or no interest.

'I understand that recently Miss Dobell has been working at Arnold Paul's house – the church organist.'

Stephanie said, 'Yes.'

'Did she ever mention her work there or discuss the Pauls?'

'I remember her saying that she liked Arnold but not his brother.'

'Did she give any reason?'

'She said they were very different.'

'Do you know the brothers?'

'I know Arnold because I attend church and I belong to the Musical Society but I have never, to my knowledge, seen his brother.'

'One more question, Mrs Vinter: did either of you go out yesterday evening?'

'My husband was out and about on the farm.'

'Apart from that?'

'No, we were at home the whole evening.'

Wycliffe was standing, not tempted by the wicker chair a second time, and now he decided that he had got as far as he was likely to without more ammunition.

He thanked them. 'I shall leave DS Lane here. After she has finished with the desk she will look over Miss Dobell's room and, perhaps, other parts of the house. We are anxious to get some sort of picture of Miss Dobell, the kind of person she was, and the life she led. Obviously you and your husband can be helpful so there may be many more questions.'

Wycliffe was looking out of the window at a romantic water-colourist's dream. It was high tide; the inlet was flooded and the overhanging trees were reflected in still water. The prow of a sizeable craft just obtruded into the picture, painted black with the gunwale lined in white.

'That boat, is it anything to do with the farm?'

'It's a houseboat; a man called Lavin and a boy live on it and pay rent to the farm for the berth. The man is badly disfigured and rarely leaves the boat.'

'Is there a path along the river bank back to the village?'

'If you don't mind mud over your ankles.'

She saw him to the front door and he was about to leave when a slim, blond youth, dressed in jeans and a denim jacket, came up the grassy slope which separated the house from the water. Slung over his shoulder he carried a pair of binoculars in a much-worn leather case. The boy eyed him with a certain hostility and did not acknowledge his casual greeting, but the expression on Stephanie's face answered his unspoken question as to what might ruffle her calm or raise her emotional temperature.

'The path leads off on your right.'

Mother and son went into the house and the door closed behind them.

He walked down the slope which ended in a low bank and a narrow strip of shingle. The path gathered itself together out of the shingle and was lost to sight almost at once as it rounded a bend where the inlet joined the river. He could see the boat now – a houseboat with a superstructure covering most of the deck. Wycliffe prided himself that, after more than twenty years living by the sea, he had learned enough to identify this craft as a former fishing boat of that vaguely defined species called 'luggers' from the sails they are built to carry. She was well maintained, the hull painted black, with a white superstructure, and varnished, hardwood windows.

Smoke came from a cowled stove-pipe; curtains were drawn across the windows, and he saw no-one but, looking back, he glimpsed a man's bearded face peering after him from between the curtains. There was a canoe, hitched by its painter to the stern of the boat.

Along the path the going was muddy and there were brown pools, but nowhere did water or mud reach his ankles. Shortly after leaving the house he had the river on his left and an area of reedy marsh on his right. A great place for birds. Even now there were swans and at least three different sorts of duck on the water. He knew nothing about ducks and decided that he would learn.

It was very quiet. When, close by, some creature plopped into the water it had almost the impact of a shot. Here in this narrow valley, between wooded banks, evening came early and he found himself hurrying as though to overtake the dusk. In the back of his mind he was brooding on the dead woman and on her way of life. He felt sure that the farmhouse had changed hardly at all since that day, many years ago, when her parents set out on their ill-fated coach trip – or for years before that. He asked himself: how many women of Jessica's generation would have shown such apparent indifference to comfort and convenience?

Lucy Lane's verdict would be enlightening.

In a surprisingly short space of time he had arrived where the churchyard bordered the river and there was a kissing-gate. He could continue along the river bank to the village or he could go up through the churchyard. He decided to leave the path and look in at the church.

Lucy Lane found little of interest in the roll-top desk: invoices and receipts and a simple account book recording farming transactions, copies of returns sent to the Ministry, a few letters concerning the farm, nothing personal . . . There were the minimum records which, processed on the cheap by some shrewd, old-fashioned book-keeper, would serve to keep the tax dragon at bay and claim all the subsidies on offer.

In one of the pigeon-holes she came across a chunky, hard-covered, well-thumbed manuscript book labelled 'Farm Diary' and she leafed through it. Jessica had made systematic but telegraphic entries about seed-sowing, planting, spreading fertilizer and goat-kidding – there was not, as far as she could see, a single entry of a personal nature.

She turned to Vinter. 'Now I want to look at Miss Dobell's bedroom and I would like you or Mrs Vinter to come with me.'

Vinter was sullen. 'It's nothing to do with us.'

But Stephanie said, 'I'll come up with you.'

In the bedroom Lucy opened drawers and peered into the wardrobe. She was impressed, as Wycliffe had been, by the characterless nature of the room, and by the fact that in all probability it had been the same for fifty years at least. Stored away in the chest were unused sheets and blankets which must have been new in Jessica's grandmother's day, and when the drawers were opened the stench of mothballs filled the room. The window was small and tightly shut so that one seemed cut off from the river and the world outside.

Jessica's clothes were incidental: several pairs of jeans, a couple of skirts, two or three jumpers, a blouse or two and a random selection of underclothes.

It was depressing. Stephanie, watching from the doorway, was ironic. 'Clothes were hardly Jessica's main interest in life.'

'But didn't she have anything personal? What did interest her other than the farm?'

A faint smile. 'If she had another interest I never discovered it – unless it was men.'

'Didn't she receive any letters other than business ones?'

'I've no idea.'

Lucy was becoming irritated by the woman's smug detachment. 'But you must have seen whatever the postman brought.'

'No. There's a mailbox by the gate which she kept locked. She emptied it herself and handed over whatever concerned us.'

Finally Lucy looked under the bed and was rewarded by a metal deed box which she dragged out. 'Did you know about this?'

Stephanie raised her shoulders but said nothing.

The box was not locked and she spread its contents on the honeycomb quilt: a small, shaggy teddy bear with a squeak; a cheap camera at least twenty years old; a photograph album and a few items of jewellery, wrapped in tissue paper, presumably her mother's. Finally Lucy brought out a small number of envelopes held together by an elastic band.

The envelopes caught Lucy's attention; she sensed a find. There were three; they had been through the mail and carried recent postmarks, the latest, no more than a week ago. They were cheap, business envelopes and were addressed in carefully distorted block capitals, the badge of those who, for some reason, wish to appear illiterate as well as anonymous.

Lucy slipped a single sheet of lined paper from one of them. In the middle of the otherwise blank page was a biblical quotation, written in the same block capitals as the address: 'Thou hast played the harlot with many lovers – Jeremiah: 3:1.'

Lucy was intrigued. It struck her as slightly mad. A daughter of the manse she was nevertheless a child of the sixties and, for her, anonymous admonishment by way of biblical texts belonged to the same epoch as the Salem witch trials. She was tempted, but restrained her curiosity about the other envelopes, knowing that Fox would not welcome her prints being added to any others there might be.

'Did you know she was getting anonymous letters?'

'I knew that she'd had one.'

'Did she tell you?'

'I was there when she opened it. It must have been about a fortnight ago. She had come in with the mail – three or four items, she glanced through them and held up one envelope addressed in pencil and in block capitals. She said, "See this? Somebody who doesn't like me." She slit open the envelope, removed a sheet of paper, glanced at it, showed it to me, and said, "Silly cow!"'

'Did you get the impression she knew who had sent it?'

'I got that impression – yes.'

'She gave you no hint?'

'No.'

Lucy said: 'I must take these – and the photograph album. I'll give you a receipt.'

Family photographs are a good source of background. Everything else went back into the box.

It was downstairs as Lucy was leaving that Stephanie thawed. At the last moment it seemed that she was reluctant to break off contact with another woman. 'You probably think that we are unfeeling, but if you had lived as we have for the past three years . . . You see, neither Laurence nor I had any experience of this kind of life . . . But it wasn't only that.' She paused, then added, 'Jessica was a hard woman. Of course we should never have come here.'

'What did you do before?'

'I was a librarian, I have a degree in English. Of course I made the mistake of giving it up when I married – and lost my independence. Laurence had visions of us doing some literary work together while he carried on with his job, but nothing came of it.' She blinked, and her blue eyes misted over. 'Recently, I've been spending some time at Trecara, helping to catalogue Carey's library . . . Are you married?'

'No.'

'Sensible woman . . . Ah, well, Giles is my future.'

Chapter Four

Easter Sunday evening

In the churchyard the rooks were cawing, coming home to roost. Wycliffe entered the church by the south porch. A uniformed policeman stood guard.

'No sightseers?'

'They got tired, sir. But the press have been – and gone. Mr Kersey dealt with them.'

Just inside, on the table where the visitors' book and offertory box were normally kept, Fox and his assistant were logging their treasure trove: little envelopes, each with its tag; the hammer, an ordinary hammer except for its long handle; rolls of film; a clutch of scale diagrams . . .

A grumbling noise from the tower warned that the clock was about to strike and Wycliffe counted the seven strokes almost in disbelief. Fox had taken away his floodlamps, the lighting was dim, the church was returning to normal. Evidence of its desecration had been removed, the flowers were as fragrant as ever, and the statue of Christ looked out across the chancel steps, lantern held high.

'Anything, Fox?'

Fox, excessively lean and lanky, brooded over and fiddled with his hoard like a fastidious stork arranging and rearranging its nest material. Asking him a question was like interrogating a computer, one had to get him into the right mode first. After the necessary lapse of time he said, 'Large numbers of prints, sir, but I've no way of knowing at the moment whose. The weapon was wiped clean, so were the organ keys and the blower switch.'

'You've got the bits of card used to wedge the keys?'

'Pieces of printed paper, sir, neatly cut and folded. They came from a magazine.'

'Any indication which?'

'A religious magazine, but there are several and I shall have to check them out.' Fox produced a block plan of the chancel and the adjacent area including the organ. 'I found a few flakes of mud, sir – river mud, I think, on the carpet of the south aisle. I've marked them with an M on the plan.'

The distribution of the flakes suggested that someone with muddy footwear had walked from the south porch towards the chancel. It was obviously possible that the mud had come from the feet of the killer and that he or she had reached the church by the river bank. The vicar had only to cross the road from his vicarage.

Fox went on, 'I found no actual footprint but one of the flakes carried an impression of the toe of what was probably a rubber boot. It was too fragile to take a cast but I've got photographs.'

'Good. Is Mr Kersey about?'

'I think he must be; I saw him a few minutes ago.'

Wycliffe found Kersey studying an inscribed tablet set in the wall of the chancel. Kersey read aloud: 'Thou shalt not kill, Thou shalt not commit adultery, Thou shalt not steal, Thou shalt not bear false witness . . .' And he added, 'That little lot adds up to our meal ticket.'

Wycliffe grinned. 'I'd be quite willing to take early retirement. Anyway, what's new? I hear you've had the press.'

'A reporter from the Plymouth paper with his cameraman, another from the local, and an agency chap.'

'Did you let them in?'

'Yes. The body had gone and Fox was all but through. I kept 'em up the west end, away from the chancel area, but they got their pictures.'

'Any good news?'

'Shaw has found us a home, an old school building just off the square, only recently vacated. The Central Stores people are fitting it out. Lucy Lane has laid on a house-to-house: the last time anybody saw Jessica; whether anybody was spotted entering or leaving the churchyard last evening . . . Actually, anybody could get in or out almost anywhere along the boundary wall. There's even a footpath and a kissing-gate down by the waterside.'

'I know. What happens here when Fox has finished?'

'The vicar has agreed to us putting seals on the place for the time being. Incidentally, Tom Reed has gone back to his burrow but we know where to find him.'

'I didn't get any lunch; did you?'

'No, and I'm beginning to miss it. Let's look in at the pub, sir, they must do some sort of evening meal. Ted Shaw did a bit of prospecting there earlier and it's got the Shaw Seal of Approval.'

The Hopton Arms was in the square by the post office, on the corner of Church Lane. Its sign carried a colourful portrait of the old royalist general on one side, and his achievement of arms on the other. The windows were diamond paned, there was a bit of fake timbering, and a rustic board, inscribed in Gothic lettering, offered meals and accommodation.

Kersey said, 'It's a bit olde worlde and the food probably comes out of a microwave but if the beer is reasonable I can live with that.'

Inside, the bar was at one end of a long room, cluttered with the usual furniture, tables with plastic tops that looked like marble and shiny wooden chairs that looked like plastic. At the far end, above glass doors, was a sign with the word 'Restaurant' in blue neon light and, beyond the doors, guarded by a couple of rubber plants, tables with blue cloths were laid, ready for the evening meal. Apart from the landlord, and three or four regulars drinking at the bar, the place was empty.

'Chief Superintendent Wycliffe and Inspector Kersey; am I right?' The landlord came from behind the bar, holding out his hand. He was a big man with short, dark curly hair; he wore a Yacht Club jersey and blue denim trousers. 'Johnny Glynn, at your service. Everybody calls me Johnny. Your Mr Shaw, who was here earlier, made provisional bookings for both of you, and for a DS Lane.'

Wycliffe growled and Kersey said, 'What's your draught bitter like?'

'You shall try it, gentlemen – on the house.'

The pints were drawn and the landlord stood watching while they were sampled. 'Well?'

Kersey said, 'It's good bitter, I'll give you that.'

The landlord glanced up at the clock. 'We serve meals from eight on Sundays; seven-thirty on other days; menus on the tables.'

Wycliffe inquired, 'Why Hopton?'

Johnny grinned. 'Royalist general in the Civil War, he met General Fairfax of the parliamentary lot on Tresillian Bridge, not far from here, to agree terms for ending the war in Cornwall. That was March 1646, and legend says he slept here.' Johnny shrugged. 'Could be true, and it might have been good for trade once; now if you said the Virgin Mary slept here they'd want to know "Who's she?" It's the new education.'

Wycliffe picked up his glass, Kersey had his refilled, and they moved away from the bar to seats at one of the little tables. It was dusk, and the lights were switched on.

Kersey said, 'That landlord is a bit of a pain but the

place is all right.' Changing the subject, he went on, 'So you've been to the farm, sir . . . ?'

Wycliffe studied the bottom of his glass but refused a refill. 'The dead woman – Jessica . . . Imagine a girl in her very early twenties, her parents killed in a coach crash . . . She insists on keeping the family farm going and, for seventeen years, she succeeds more or less, sometimes going out to work to make ends meet . . .'

'A determined young woman.'

'You can say that again.'

Wycliffe was still struggling to come to grips with the personality of the victim; trying to assess what he had gleaned from his visit to the farm.

'That little house . . . It's spartan. Either she was indifferent to creature comforts or she had a pretty broad streak of self-denial. The family who lived with her had a bleak time, that's for sure.'

Kersey finished his beer. Knowing from experience what this was all about, he asked the right questions: 'What are they like?'

Wycliffe grimaced. 'The man was a lecturer – Bristol – modern languages, but had a breakdown. Academic . . . Well-intentioned, probably hard working, but there's something . . . A square peg doomed to find himself in round holes, and resenting it.'

'And the woman?'

'Ornamental, probably well educated . . . musical. I'd guess not much of a clue when it comes to things like earning a living or organizing anything more complicated than tea and biscuits for the vicar.'

Wycliffe twisted his empty glass on a beer mat. 'Anyway, we should have the Lane version shortly. I left her there to snoop around and arrange for their statements. By the way, I want you to make inquiries about Vinter – why, precisely, did he give up his job? It shouldn't be difficult, it was only three or four years ago. And, while you're about it, you might check him out with CRO.'

Kersey lit a cigarette. 'You think he might have form?'

'How should I know? I'm simply trying to size him up; he made me feel uncomfortable.'

Kersey waited, but no more came. Time to prime the pump: 'And our Jessie got herself murdered, so there must have been emotional dynamite around somewhere.'

'Exactly. Presumably a man. Jessica was sometimes away all night; on two occasions, two nights running.'

'No explanation offered?'

'None.'

Kersey said, 'All the same, it's difficult to square the staging and the props with any kind of sex killing I've ever come across.'

Wycliffe nodded. 'It's hard to square any sort of killing, sexual or otherwise, with that theatrical set-up in the church. I've never met anything quite like it. Killing somebody against that background to the accompaniment of five notes which Schumann strung together to flatter his girlfriend – all played at once . . . There's a dangerous dottiness . . .'

People were drifting in, ordering drinks at the bar and taking them through the glass doors to the dining tables in the restaurant. They came mainly in couples but there was one party of five or six. 'You'll have to push the tables together tonight, Johnny; Gemma's got a birthday – her twenty-ninth.'

A wag called, 'Hey up, Gemma! You had that one last year.'

Lucy Lane arrived, an attractive, youngish woman on her own, and a stranger. She was watched, and there was obvious surprise when she joined the two middle-aged men at one of the bar tables. Only the better informed knew they were from the police.

Lucy, taken into the squad as a gesture to sexual equality, had quickly established herself in the hierarchy and she had side-stepped promotion because her next move would have taken her out of CID.

'I hope I did the right thing, sir? I suggested to Ted Shaw that it might be a good idea to make a provisional booking here.'

Wycliffe said, 'I'll tell you in the morning. Do you know what he's doing with the others?'

'They've been fixed up by sub-division: a small, private hotel in Truro; transport has been laid on.'

'I think we'd better find a table.'

But the landlord had already reserved one in a corner by the window.

'Will the hock suit you?'

'What's Chicken à la Marengo?'

'I'm not keen on mushrooms.'

'You'll have to put up with 'em if you have that.'

Meanwhile the party atmosphere was warming up. It seemed that everybody knew everybody else and apparently meaningless sallies raised gusts of laughter and fresh banter from around the tables.

The meal was served by two waitresses from a kitchen, seen through an open door, where a fat woman in a white coat did things with pans on a stove. No microwave in sight. Johnny, the landlord, moved from table to table.

'Everything to your liking, madam, and sirs?'

Wycliffe said, 'Is it always like this?'

'Not every night – this is about usual for Wednesdays and Sundays, they're our busy nights. Perhaps they're a bit more subdued than usual tonight because of Jessica.'

Kersey said, 'Nobody would notice.'

Wycliffe asked, 'Was the dead woman in on these occasions?'

'She didn't come here.'

'And the Geaches?'

The landlord's mobile features were suddenly expressionless. 'No.'

Gemma's health was drunk around the tables and they sang 'Happy Birthday to You', but with the arrival of the cheeseboard and coffee, things began to quieten down.

'Well, what did you make of the farm, Lucy?'

Lucy Lane, as always, took time to consider. 'I don't know about the farm, but the house is a museum piece – as you saw. The dead woman intrigues me: all that scraping and saving and going out to work, just to keep going. Incidentally, she kept a farm diary but there's nothing in it of a personal nature that I can see. I brought it away with me just in case.'

After placing a fragment of cheese on a water biscuit and nibbling it, she went on: 'Jessica was getting anonymous letters – or notes, three in the past two months. I handed them over to Fox, still in their envelopes, but I looked at one. It accused her of being a harlot, in a quotation from the Bible. Fox has promised to have them processed, with copies, by the morning.'

Wycliffe said, 'That's all we need! Anyway, what was your impression of the Vinters?'

A wrinkled brow. 'I think I got her measure, sir, but I'm not so sure about him. Stephanie has a degree in English; she was a librarian before she married, and recently she's been spending two or three afternoons a week at Trecara Manor – that's the house with the folly – helping to catalogue Carey's library. I don't suppose she gets paid for that. She doesn't seem a bad sort and I may sound catty, but I doubt if Stephanie has ever felt under any obligation to earn a living.'

'And Vinter?'

'As I said; he's a different case. Not much of what goes on inside shows. Seven-tenths, or whatever, submerged.'

'A possible killer?'

Some hesitation, then, 'If I asked you that question, sir, I'd get short shrift.'

Wycliffe grinned. 'But?'

'I felt there was something, but I couldn't put my finger on it.'

Wycliffe turned to Kersey. 'We've already agreed, that's one for you, Doug: some background on Vinter. Lecturer to labourer in one jump calls for explanation. He mentioned a breakdown but we need to know what kind. It shouldn't be difficult.'

Kersey emptied his coffee cup and sat back. 'That was a good meal.'

Wycliffe refused more coffee and said, 'I think I'll take a walk.'

Predictable; that was his routine when away from home: after the evening meal, a solitary walk, a telephone call to Helen, then bed.

Outside it was chilly, and he fetched a coat from his car, still parked in the square. It occurred to him that he ought to look in at the newly established Incident Room before indulging his whim. DS Shaw would have worked the usual minor miracle and deserved at least a paternal pat.

He found the former school, tucked away behind the post office in the middle of its asphalt playground: traditional Cornish, circa 1900, a single-storied, twin-gabled building of grey stone with granite coigns. Although small, it had two doors, one with 'Girls and Infants', the other 'Boys' carved in the granite lintels. The girls' door was open, and lit. A board propped on the steps carried a poster: 'Police Incident Room', and a uniformed PC said, 'The room on the left, sir.'

The former classroom, separated from another by the usual glass screen, was clean, well-lit, and would probably be almost cosy when the two bottled-gas heaters were working. Furniture and equipment disgorged by Central Stores was being arranged and installed by police personnel, while British Telecom chalked up Sunday overtime. Boxes of stationery were stacked on the floor and a bevy of VDUs, lined against the wall, yearned blankly for partnership with their electronic keyboards. Shaw looked upon his work and saw that it was not so bad, and getting better.

'There's a lady here, sir – Mrs Geach – sister of the dead woman. She insisted on waiting to see you though I told her it was by no means certain you would be in. I put her in the interview room.'

The 'interview room' turned out to be a former store cupboard with a tiny window. It now had a table and two chairs but such is the power of a name that Wycliffe at once recognized and accepted its role. Even the smell seemed to be right. The woman stood up as Wycliffe came in.

'Katherine Geach – Jessica's sister. I thought you would have come to the house . . .' Her manner was accusing.

'Superintendent Wycliffe.' He mumbled the introduction, sounding apologetic. God knows why except that the woman was strikingly good looking, with restless dark eyes. She was obviously distressed.

He tried sympathy but without effect. Her hands, clasped tightly together, rested on the table top. 'You know that my sister worked part-time for Arnold Paul – the organist at the church?'

'He told me.'

'So you've talked to him! You know that he has his brother living with him?'

'I understand that is fairly recent.'

'Yes.'

Suddenly she seemed to have run out of steam; she had been rehearsing what she would say for too long, now she had to stop and think. 'Yesterday morning – Saturday – my sister came to see me . . .'

'Is that unusual?' asked Wycliffe, recalling that he was a policeman.

She was pushed a little further off balance. 'Well, I suppose it is.' She made an irritable gesture. 'I don't know; the fact is that I usually go to see her rather than the other way round. Does it matter?'

'Probably not. So she came to see you?'

Hesitation. 'Well, she was in the village, shopping, and she just dropped in. She wanted to tell me about something odd which had happened at Arnold Paul's place on Friday afternoon.'

'She was worried?'

'I don't think she was worried, just intrigued.'

'Anyway, go on.' He was in the driving seat now. Mean, but necessary.

'She doesn't – didn't think that Philip – the man who came to live there – is Arnold's brother. She thought there was something crooked going on.'

'Can you enlarge on that?'

'Apparently she had heard them quarrelling more than once and sometimes Arnold called the other man "Timmy" instead of "Phil" as he usually did. Anyway, on Friday afternoon the quarrel was worse. The other man was threatening, and Arnold said, "All you'll achieve by that, my boy, is to put us both inside." There was more, but I can't remember it all.'

'They must have been very careless to let your sister overhear this.'

'They didn't know she was there; she was early, and Mabel Tripp, the old housekeeper, let her in.'

'But Mabel, herself—'

'Mabel is as deaf as a post.'

'You think this could have something to do with what happened to your sister?'

She looked down, fiddling with her handbag. 'I thought you should know, just in case.'

'Yes, you are quite right.' He suspected that there was something more, perhaps something that she found more difficult to talk about.

She looked up. 'I was wondering if I ought—'

There was a commotion outside and a man burst into the little room.

'Kathy! What the hell are you doing here? I've looked everywhere—' He broke off, and turned on Wycliffe: 'What do you mean by keeping my wife—?'

Wycliffe stood up. 'I assume that you are Mr Abe Geach. I am Detective Chief Superintendent Wycliffe. Your wife was waiting for me here when I arrived. She volunteered some information and I was about to ask her to make a formal statement. But that can wait until the morning when she has had time to think over what she has told me.'

He turned back to the woman: 'You were about to say . . . ?'

'Oh, nothing, it was of no importance.'

'In the morning, then. At the same time, Mr Geach, there are some questions I shall want to put to you, so I suggest that you are available then.'

Geach stood, rocking on the balls of his feet like a boxer. 'I've got my business to attend to in the morning.'

'No doubt, but this is a murder inquiry. I, or one of my officers, will be at Trigg sometime during the morning – unless you would prefer to come here?'

Wycliffe let his gaze rest on Geach until the silence was observable, then turned to the wife. 'Just one other matter while you are here, Mrs Geach, I understand that the farm belonged to you and your sister jointly – is there a formal agreement?'

'Yes, Jessica insisted on it. The agreement was drawn up by Harry Nicholls of Nicholls and Greet in Truro.'

'Do you know if your sister made a will?'

'We both did, leaving our interest in the farm to each other.'

'Well, thank you for coming along, Mrs Geach. I shall certinly look into what you have told me.'

Geach hesitated, then shrugged. 'Come on, Kathy; let's get out of here.'

Wycliffe was puzzled by Madam Geach. The story about Paul and his brother was probably true and might be significant but people, even the bereaved, do not usually come running to the police in such a hurry. Could Katherine really believe that her sister had been murdered in such an extraordinary way because she had overheard something incriminating from the Pauls? Or was she anxious to divert attention from nearer home?

Wycliffe returned to the square, determined not to be deprived of his walk. The square was reasonably well-lit with lights from the houses as well as a couple of street lamps, but as he walked towards the foreshore he seemed to be approaching a wall of darkness. It was only when he had left the square behind and could feel the shingle beneath his feet that he began to see the gleam of light on the water, to distinguish the shadowy banks of the creek, and the outlines of overhanging trees. Then, turning a little more to his left, he could make out the irregular roof of Trigg against the sky.

The organist, Arnold Paul, and his alleged brother: interesting. It was by no means impossible that a man who had made a good killing in some illicit deals and escaped the law should retire to a village like Moresk and find a respected place in the community. Few villains carry labels, many are neither brutish nor uncultured. Wycliffe well remembered a drugs dealer who had a reputation as a poet, and an armed bank robber who translated philosophical works from the Russian . . . Nor was it unlikely that such a man would be sought out in retirement and latched on to by another crook in need of a hideaway.

Walking along the shore, crunching over the shingle, he came upon a footpath which seemed to follow the line of the shore and to mark the boundary of Trigg land; obviously the other end of the path from the farmhouse by which he had reached the kissing-gate and the churchyard. He ventured along the path for a few yards and was surprised to find that the trees gave out and that there was open ground, across a lawn, to the house. There were lights, both upstairs and down, and Wycliffe wondered what sort of inquest was taking place there. For some reason, which he preferred not to examine, overtly sexual men like Geach stimulated his aggression.

The organist thing nagged like a sore tooth. It could be a lead, but he was dubious. Even assuming that the dead woman had overheard something deeply incriminating, how had they found out and acted with such dramatic despatch? And why the bizarre window dressing? Above all, why draw attention to the organ and, therefore, to the organist?

Wycliffe muttered to himself, out of temper, and gave up the idea of a walk. He returned to the square, collected his bag from the car, and re-entered the Hopton Arms. The tables in the restaurant were deserted and had been cleared. There were three or four people around the bar, a couple playing darts, and others scattered among the little tables nearby. Kersey was there, alone at one of them, nursing a glass of bitter.

'Lucy is having an early night. Feel like a nightcap?'

'No, I'm half asleep as it is.' He told Kersey of his interview with Katherine Geach, and of the arrival of her husband. 'One of us must go there in the morning. I shall be interested to see whether they choose to be interviewed separately or together.'

'Do you think there's anything in this business with the Paul brothers?'

'I've no idea; that's for tomorrow.' He stood up. 'Now I'm going to phone Helen, if I can find a phone in this place.'

The landlord had overheard: 'There's a pay-phone in the corridor outside the bedrooms, but if you want privacy, you can use the phone in the office.'

Wycliffe was chastened.

'It's me.'

'I thought it might be. So you're not coming home tonight.'

'No, this looks like being difficult. I'm at the Hopton Arms in Moresk Village – I'll give you the number.'

'Comfortable?'

'Seems so. The food is good.'

Just in time, he stopped himself from asking how the garden was looking, realizing that he had been away only a few hours.

'Have you been for your walk?'

'A short one.'

'Look after yourself.'

'And you. Good night.'

He went to bed, determined to put the case out of his mind, and lay awake thinking about Jessica Dobell. Her character, if anything, would provide the key; he was sure of that. And what did that amount to? Jessica – work and sex. It was like the word-association game played by psychologists. Work and sex which she pursued aggressively, with almost frenzied dedication and no regard for her own comfort or anybody else's.

One looked for an aim – an end in view. Money? Security? There were easier ways. Wycliffe felt instinctively that there was no aim, no vision of a future. But what? Could it be an obsessive concern to obliterate something that was past?

He needed to know more about her.

There was nothing wrong with his bed but he tossed and turned. Once, when he got out to recover his duvet from the floor, he looked out of the window and discovered that it was raining, a soft spring rain which sometimes comes when the wind is southerly, bringing with it the tang of a not too distant sea.

His little clock said five minutes past one. He returned to bed and, resigned to sleeplessness, fell asleep almost at once. When he awoke it was broad daylight.

For the Geaches it was a troubled night. To avoid disturbing one another they separated. Abe slept in the spare room but, shortly after daybreak, he crept into their bedroom and found Katherine wide awake. Clumsily solicitous, he came to sit on the side of the bed and stroked her hair.

'We've got to talk, Kath.'

'What is there to say?'

'The police are coming this morning and they will go on until they find out who did it.'

'Isn't that what we want?' Listless.

'Of course, but we ought to be ready to tell them certain things. I mean, they're outsiders, they didn't even know her.'

'You've got something on your mind; why not say it?'

Abe ran a hand through his dark curls. 'I don't want to upset you but think of how she was found. I mean, you *know* how she was found – you insisted on knowing. What I'm trying to say is that there must have been something in her life which explains her death – and the way of her death. That's how the police will look at it.'

'There was what she found out about Arnold's brother – as I told Wycliffe.'

'That the brother wasn't who he said he was and that they seemed to be mixed up in some shady business. Do you think they would have killed her because she overheard something of that sort? The chances are they didn't even know they'd been overheard, but even if they did, even if they decided to kill her, would they have laid on a bloody peep-show to do it?'

She was silent for a while, her dark eyes staring at the ceiling.

Geach went on: 'She must have been killed by somebody who meant to kill her and who chose to do it in that way – making a show, what they call nowadays a statement.'

'Like: "Here is a whore!" That's what you mean, isn't it? You're saying that whoever did it was warped – perverted!'

Abe said quietly, 'All right. Did she know anybody like that? . . . Do we? Or somebody who might be?'

She turned to look at him and for the first time he thought that he had her whole attention. 'You still haven't said all you want to say, Abe.'

'No, I'll say it now. Have you thought of Lavin?'

'The houseboat man!' She sat up in her astonishment. 'But Jess had nothing to do with Lavin. His boat happened to be berthed on the foreshore belonging to the farm and the rent was their only contact. He's so badly disfigured that, apart from the lad who lives with him, he doesn't see anybody. Jess hardly ever mentioned him.'

Geach was solemn. 'What you say is true, up to a point; Lavin is a recluse and most of his contacts are through the boy, but you can take it from me, Kath, Jess knew Lavin very well and she spent a lot of time with him.'

'Are you saying they were having an affair?' Her voice was hard.

Geach held out a hand to rest it on her arm. 'I've no proof that they went to bed together, but Jess and he were pretty close. I know that, and I think I should tell the police.'

'Why?'

'Why?' Geach reasoned patiently, as though with a child. 'How old is he? Forty? Not much more, and from what I've heard it's about seven years since he had his accident. God knows what goes on in the mind of a man like that, living there with only the boy for company. Career gone, family gone, friends . . . I don't know the details, but it must be something like that. Then along comes Jess – a very attractive woman, and she gives him friendship and whatever . . .'

Katherine was frowning. 'But everybody says the pair on the boat are gay.'

'Well, they would, wouldn't they? And they may be, but in Lavin's case it could well be Hobson's choice.'

Katherine tried to come to grips with this further insight into her sister's life. 'But even if what you say is true, why would he want to . . . I mean, why . . . ?' Her voice faltered.

Geach squeezed her arm. 'I know what you mean, kid. But what if, for some reason, Jess wanted to stop seeing him – to break off whatever they had between them? That's one possibility, but there's another. If there was a gay thing going between Lavin and his boyfriend there would be jealousy . . .'

'You mean it could have been the boy . . .'

'We just don't know, but we ought to put the police in the picture.'

After a long silence she looked up at him with sudden suspicion. 'How could you possibly know what you've just told me?'

He spoke quietly. 'Let's leave it that I do know it, Kath – just for now.' His manner was pleading.

She said in a toneless voice, 'All right. Just for now.'

'There's something else . . .'

'Go on.'

'About the farm. I know it's too early to talk about the long term but it's got to be kept going for the present, and without Jessica . . .'

'Well?'

'I've got a chap labouring on the Highertown site who rented a smallholding until last year when he went bust. Nothing would please him more than to get back to farming, even on a temporary basis. He could help out there.'

'Who's going to pay him?'

'He can stay on my payroll until things – well, until we know where we stand over the other business.'

Katherine swept back her hair in a tired gesture. 'I don't feel right about the "other business" as you call it, Abe. If it goes ahead now it's like taking advantage of what happened to Jess.'

Geach put his hand on her shoulder. 'Yes, well, there's no hurry to do anything. Just see how you feel as time goes on.'

Katherine looked at her husband, and was thoughtful. 'I wish I knew what was behind all this, Abe. It can wait, but don't take me for a complete fool.'

Chapter Five

Easter Monday

Lucy Lane, first down, said, 'It was the usual bacon, egg and sausage thing, or kedgeree. Johnny was anxious to get on, because of the holiday, so I said kedgeree.'

Kersey, who carried on a more or less clandestine affair with saturated fats, grumbled, 'It's as bad as being home.'

Wycliffe, more Jesuitical, preferred such decisions to be made for him. 'Kedgeree suits me.'

There were only two other tables occupied, one by an elderly, studious-looking couple who were probably touring Cornish churches or looking for ley lines; the other, by two pin-striped salesmen types who must surely have strayed off the spine road and got pixilated.

At a little before half past eight the police party left the pub for the Incident Room around the corner. In the fine, misty rain every surface shone or glistened, and every ledge dripped. Kersey stopped at the post office. 'I want some cigarettes.'

'Get a couple of newspapers at the same time.'

Despite the rain there was activity in the square; a van was unloading at the post office, a couple of cars were filling with petrol at the garage, and a boat was being hauled up the slipway. The Truro bus was about to move off, though without its usual complement of workers and shoppers. Easter Monday was a holiday for most people.

In the Incident Room order had been extracted out of

chaos. As yet it was on a small scale – just three fumble-fingered policemen tapping away on their machines. He was guided to his tiny office, leaving Kersey and Lucy Lane to sort out what was new.

Wycliffe's cubby hole had been carved out of a classroom as an office for a former headteacher. There was just room for a desk, a cupboard and a couple of chairs, and the original furniture was still there. In one of the desk drawers he found a little book recording visits by the school nurse and a pad of forms for reporting damage and dilapidations affecting buildings and equipment.

When Kersey joined him he was standing, staring out of the window at the gleaming wet asphalt of the playground and the boundary wall. He was recapturing that childhood experience of school – utterly cut off from the world, while a clock on the wall doled out some of the longest minutes and hours that he would ever know.

The two of them sat down. 'Mind if I smoke, sir?' A ritual question, but an acknowledgement of their hierarchic relationship which would probably last for the rest of the day. Kersey had the newspapers.

'Anything in them?'

Kersey pushed over the regional paper, the *Morning News*, folded back.

'They weren't in time for the national early editions we get down here, but this chap's done pretty well.'

There were two library pictures of the church: one of the exterior, the other a view of the chancel.

The headlines read: 'Murder in Church', 'Ritual Killing?'. And the text went on: 'When the Reverend Michael Jordan, Vicar of Moresk, arrived to celebrate Holy Communion at his church on the morning of Easter day he found the partly clothed body of Jessica Dobell, sprawled across the chancel steps, at the very feet of a statue of Christ. She had been brutally killed by a blow to the head, believed to have been inflicted by a hammer found close to her body.'

The wedged organ keys were said to provide: 'a distressing, nerve-jangling discord as an accompaniment to this scene of horror which confronted the vicar.

'It is difficult to see this crime as other than a bizarre and senseless ritual murder.'

Wycliffe said, 'That should bring 'em down by the car load. Anything more helpful in our own reports?'

'Nothing factual. Nobody was seen entering or leaving the church on Saturday evening or, if they were, it was so ordinary that the fact didn't register. Of course, we now have formal statements from the vicar and from the Vinters – including the boy.'

'What about gossip?'

'Jessica isn't getting quite the flattering obituary the victim can usually count on. There's some talk of her meanness, more of her sex life. No names, but it won't be difficult to ferret them out when the dust has settled a bit. It seems that the Women's Guild, under the presidency of the vicar's sister, resented Jessica having the church cleaning job – not that anybody else wanted it, but she was regarded as morally tainted.'

'The Vinters?'

Kersey brushed ash from his shirt front. 'Vinter is rarely seen in the village but he often goes to church with his wife on Sunday evenings. It seems he's interested in natural history – especially bats, and he's doing some sort of survey. Stephanie belongs to the Musical Society, run by the vicar and the organist. She's regarded as a kind of phenomenon, not quite real.'

Kersey's lined features contorted into one of his baby-frighteners, registering mirth. 'One woman said she didn't get taken down and dusted often enough. The boy, Giles, belonged to the Musical Society but gave up a month or two back, though he still goes to church with his parents. He's got the name for being a big-head. Seems he's something of a prodigy at school; a sound bet for the Oxbridge scholarship stakes.'

'Anything on the Geaches?'

'Another slice of family life. Geach's father died of a heart attack in his early sixties. Mother Geach is still around; she shares a harbour flat at Falmouth with another widow. Abe carries on where his father left off, a workaholic, and is expected to go the same way as his dad. He's also got a name as a womanizer. His contracts take him all over the two counties and he uses a rather plush motor-caravan as a mobile office and sleeping quarters. Useful for his women too.'

'Any suggestion of local women being involved?'

'One doorstep oracle hinted at Jessica – I suppose that was inevitable; but she backed down when pressed.'

'Paul and his brother?'

'Arnold Paul is well liked but so are most people who give away money. Nobody seems to have seen much of the brother.'

Wycliffe brooded. 'I think I'll see the Pauls while you have a go at the Geaches. Turn the screw a bit if you have to.'

Lucy Lane arrived with a handful of polythene envelopes and Jessica's photograph album. 'The originals of the anonymous notes, sir. The envelopes and the sheets have been kept separate. Fox has given them the treatment; plenty of prints on the envelopes but only the dead woman's on the sheets. Whoever sent them knew enough for that.'

Lucy laid them on the desk in front of Wycliffe. 'They are in order and the dates range over the past seven weeks.'

Wycliffe looked them over with a jaundiced eye, then

began to read them aloud: 'The first one says: "Thou shalt not play the harlot – Hosea 3:3." The second: "Thou hast played the harlot with many lovers – Jeremiah 3:1." And the last: "Thou hast played the harlot with them yet couldest not be satisfied – Ezekiel 16:28." A consistent theme.'

Kersey grinned. 'And spot on. I didn't realize the Bible was up to it.'

Lucy said, 'It's all there if you're prepared to look for it, but I can't imagine why anyone would go to the trouble of sending the things. What did they expect to achieve?'

Kersey shrugged. 'What do Jehovah's Witnesses expect to achieve when they come knocking on my door? Even the sight of me doesn't put 'em off. As to who sent these, I expect there are one or two members of the Women's Guild not averse to brooding on the sex life of an unenlightened sister. A spot of reforming propaganda might seem in order.'

Wycliffe agreed. 'Yes, propaganda is the word – these don't threaten. If the sender intended violence I would expect a more aggressive follow-up to these. Surely anybody playing God would get a kick out of threatening the wrath to come before proceeding to execution.'

Lucy said, 'Perhaps, but the fact remains, Jessica is dead – murdered, and these messages were sent to her.'

There was no answer to that, so Wycliffe shuffled the plastic envelopes together and handed them back. 'All right, stir the pond Lucy, and see what comes to the surface. Now, what's this photo album?'

He turned the pages: the Dobell girls, from nappies to school uniform, on to gangling adolescence and the first flush of maturity. In the earlier photographs parents were much in evidence, in the later ones, girlfriends and boyfriends took their place. At home Helen treasured a similar record of their own twins.

Lucy drew his attention to a snapshot taken on a beach, the sea in the background; the two girls skittish in bikinis, and two boys in trunks. They faced the camera, arms linked in pairs. 'Recognize the boys, sir?'

On close inspection he recognized the one with Katherine, a younger version of Abe Geach, the contractor, lusty, brawny and ready to go. 'I can't place the other.'

Kersey said, 'You should never have been a copper, sir. That's Johnny Glynn, our sneaky landlord. He looks a good deal thinner and a lot less smug.'

The sequence came to an abrupt end with several highly professional photographs of Katherine's wedding, a very up-market occasion. Then no more photographs. The wedding, or something else at about that time, seemed to mark the end of an era for the girls. The last two or three pages of the album had been used to paste in news clippings from the local paper.

Lucy said: 'The last is recent – just a few days ago.'

'Anything particular strike you about them?'

'They're a mixed bag. Of course the report of her sister's wedding is there and an account of the inquest on their parents and the coach crash.'

'Nothing significant? – Odd?'

Lucy was hesitant. 'Not odd exactly but it happens that three of the cuttings, including the most recent one, refer to a family called Ruse from Tresillian. In January seventy-six their fifteen-year-old son was killed in a hit-and-run while cycling home. There is a report of the accident, and of the inquest which recorded a verdict of unlawful killing against a person or persons unknown.'

'A bit unorthodox.'

'Yes. Anyway, the latest cutting is an account of the funeral, last week, of the boy's mother, aged fifty-five. I wondered why that family and the incident had such obvious interest for Jessica.'

Most of police time in any investigation is spent chasing shadows but the Yorkshire Ripper case reminded every CID chief of Sod's law – that it's the shadow you don't chase which turns out to be flesh and blood.

'Find out a bit about it – don't spend too much time. The original case will be in the files so have a word with Inspector Reed; he should be able to brief you.'

He turned to Kersey. 'Now, Doug, you're for the Geaches, and I'm for the Pauls.'

But, left alone, he continued to sit at his desk, assiduously manicuring his nails with a matchstick, a habit Helen deplored.

So. Anonymous messages had been added to the elaborate charade in the church. But he knew better than to be fooled by the decoration on the cake. Underneath he would find the usual drama of jealousy or hatred or greed, or any of them in combination; a drama with a scenario little different from many others. The difference in this case was that the theme had been so overlaid; so decorated and contrived that it was unrecognizable. A hint of madness? Perhaps; but madness allied to the logic of Alice's Wonderland.

He was on the point of leaving when Potter came in: 'The boy wants to see you, sir – the Vinter boy.'

'Send him in.'

Giles Vinter came in, looking about him with apparent interest, head held back because his glasses were halfway down his nose.

'Did you ever go to this school?'

'No. I was fourteen when my parents came here and I went straight to the senior school in Truro.' The blue eyes were solemn but there was no sign of unease as he took the seat Wycliffe offered.

'Can I help you? Or, perhaps, you can help me. I assume this is about Miss Dobell?'

But Giles needed none of the routine treatment for young witnesses. The glasses were pushed up with the middle finger of the left hand, an unconscious movement. 'I didn't like her. I am not upset about her death, but I don't want you to suspect the wrong person.'

'Can you help me to suspect the right one?'

'No, but I can tell you something I didn't tell you at first. On Saturday evening there was a telephone call for her after she left for the church.'

'Any idea of the time?'

He looked thoughtful. 'I was up in my room and my parents were downstairs talking. I think they were quarrelling, and I heard my father go out – he usually goes out between eight and half-past so it must have been about then. I was coming downstairs when the telephone rang; my mother wasn't in the living room so I answered it.'

'Go on.'

'It was a man's voice, he didn't give his name, he just asked to speak to Miss Dobell. I told him she was out and he asked if I knew where he might contact her. I told him she would be at the church. He thanked me and rang off. That was all.'

'You didn't recognize the voice?'

'No.'

'Would you if you heard it again?'

'I don't think so; it was quite ordinary and we were always getting calls for her.'

'Did he give you the impression that he was worried or annoyed?'

'I don't think so.'

'I would like you to put what you have said into a fresh statement.'

'All right.'

'Before you do, just one or two more points: you said that you disliked Miss Dobell.'

'Yes; she was cruel, and she treated my mother very badly.'

'What about you and your father?'

'That too, but it was worse for my mother.'

The boy sat opposite Wycliffe, a slight figure, his blond hair cut short with a fringe, his head tilted back slightly to cope with his bifocals. He seemed self-contained and totally at ease. Wycliffe tried to draw him into talk: 'You used to belong to the church Musical Society but you gave it up . . .'

'They didn't want me.'

'I hear that you are working for your A-levels and an Oxbridge scholarship; do you think you'll make it?'

'If I decide to go ahead with it.'

'You think that you may not?'

'I don't know.'

'Do you play any games?'

'Only chess; no field games.'

'You play chess at home with your father?'

'He's no good at it. Mother plays with me sometimes, but it's not a woman's game.'

Wycliffe gave up. 'Well, thank you for coming. If you go into the next room someone will take your statement.'

Wycliffe felt deflated. But what the boy had told him might mean something. Had the killer telephoned to make sure that Jessica would be at the church? It was possible.

Before leaving for the Pauls' he studied the 1/2500 Ordnance map. Wycliffe's attitude to maps was ambivalent, even whimsical; they were a necessary evil but they diminished his world. Unless it was essential, he preferred not to know what was around the next corner or over the next hill. But here, on this single sheet of paper, all the secrets of the neighbourhood were laid bare, the village,

Trigg, the church, the path along the river bank, even the reed bed and the tower . . . No wonder people climb mountains and go to Greenland.

A century ago Moresk had consisted of a few cottages, Trigg House, the church and Trecara. The growth of Truro, the desire of shopkeepers and professional people to move 'out of town', and the fashion for second homes, combined to produce an overgrown village, lacking much coherence, but still a pleasant place to live.

The more prestigious villas were in Church Lane, on the other side from the church, and it was in one of these, behind a tall dry-stone wall topped with flowering shrubs, that Arnold Paul had settled in his retirement. Wycliffe arrived there at about ten; it was still raining but there was a pearly brightness in the sky with a promise of sun.

As he stood on the doorstep he could hear music – one of Wagner's blockbusters – he neither knew nor cared which. After some delay the doorbell was answered by Mabel, lean, angular, and no-nonsense. Because he shouted, or because she read his lips, she understood his purpose.

'You'd better come in.'

He was shown into a large room in which the senses were drowned under a welter of sound.

'You'll have to wait; he's still in the bathroom. You can sit down, but you mustn't touch things; he's fussy.'

Wycliffe traced the source of the music to a space-age, slim-line music centre in one section of which a compact disc spun smoothly, and in deceptive innocence, while feeding its coded barrage of sound to two columnar speakers, strategically placed in the room. Any means of volume control eluded him.

Having met the well-groomed, precise, and rotund

organist, who looked like Trollope's Mr Harding, Wycliffe was surprised by the comfortably relaxed and untidy room. Shelves covering most of one wall were stacked with what seemed to be musical scores; shelves on another wall held a little library of books on musicology, wedged in anyhow. Framed portraits of composers found space where there were no shelves, and any convenient ledge supported its dusty plaster bust of some eminent musician.

The point was made that Arnold Paul was a musician.

Despite the ear-splitting noise Wycliffe had not had time to get bored before Paul came in looking more than ever like a well-heeled clergyman in mufti.

'Ah, Mr Wycliffe! The music is rather loud I'm afraid, but I like to hear it in my bath.' He picked up a remote control device and silence came with the impact of a negative thud.

'There! Now, how can I help you?' He sat in one of the several armchairs, crossed his short legs, and was all attention.

'I had hoped to see your brother also.'

'My brother?' A look of surprise. 'I'm sorry, but that isn't possible; he left early this morning.'

'Left? Where did he go?'

Paul seemed slightly put out by the abruptness of the question but he put a good face on it. 'He took the seven twenty-one train to London. I ran him into Truro while I was still only half awake.'

'A sudden decision?'

'Not really.' Paul uncrossed his legs and went on with exaggerated patience: 'My brother and I do not get on well together and recently there has been increased friction. Last week it reached something of a climax and we agreed that it would be better to revert to the old arrangement under which we lived apart.'

'So, where has he gone?'

Paul was brusque. 'If you are asking me for his address, I don't know it. Probably he has booked in at some hotel while he looks around for a place that will suit him.'

'Presumably he has some sort of business?'

The little man shifted irritably in his chair. 'I know nothing of my brother's business, Mr Wycliffe! And, quite frankly, I do not understand your interest.'

'Perhaps you will give me his former address?'

Paul spread his hands. 'I cannot do that. We were in touch only by telephone until he came here and it was always he who made contact. To be frank, when he wanted something.'

'His first name is Philip?'

Paul's little eyes were alert and guarded. 'Yes, but really—'

'But you sometimes addressed him as "Timmy".'

A slight start of surprise. 'You are well informed, Mr Wycliffe. Timmy was a sort of pet name he picked up as a child. I have no idea of its origin.'

Arnold Paul was not easily put off balance but there had been a significant delay before he offered his explanation. Not that what he said was improbable.

'Your brother is younger than you?'

'By two years.'

'You were overheard to say, during one of your disagreements: "All that would achieve is to put us both inside".'

A faint smile. 'Did I say that? That would have been in connection with his suggestion for a joint business venture – a rather bitter joke on my part, I'm afraid.'

'Your brother's business activities were on the wrong side of the law?'

Another smile, a little more nervous. 'Sometimes, perhaps in a grey area; in any case, not the kind of thing in which I would want to be involved.'

'What is, or was, your business, Mr Paul?'

'I was the financial director of the London and Midlands Credit and Investment Bank.' Distant.

'You retired early?'

'I was just fifty. Music has always been my real interest and I worked hard for thirty years so that I could make it my sole concern. I could, of course, have taken it up as a career, but I knew that my talent was insufficient to earn me, as a professional musician, the kind of money I needed to keep me in comfort and security.' A smile. 'You see, Mr Wycliffe, I have never been one for starving in an attic.'

'When did you last see Jessica Dobell?'

The sudden question brought him up short. He shifted uncomfortably in his chair. 'Oh, dear! I have been rather dreading that question. There is something I should have told you, or someone, earlier. I saw her in the church on Saturday evening. I store quite a lot of music in a cupboard behind the organ and I wanted—'

'You have a key to the church?'

'Certainly! I sometimes go across to play for my own amusement and, of course, there is the Musical—'

'Who else has a key, apart from the vicar?'

'Jessica had one, and Harry Clemens, the church-warden – he owns the post office and general store in the square. Oh, and whoever is in charge of the flowers for the week.'

'What time was it when you saw Jessica?'

'About eight? At any rate between half-past seven and eight.'

'Someone telephoned the farm to speak to Jessica between eight and half-past. Was it you?'

'Why would I telephone her? I told you I have my own key.'

'What was she doing when you arrived?'

Paul hesitated as though the next bit would be even more difficult.

'There is a door off the chancel into the vestry which closes on a spring and a wooden wedge keeps it open when required. Someone had wedged it too securely and Jessica was trying to free it by knocking it gently with a hammer.'

'With a hammer.' Wycliffe's voice was bleak.

'I'm afraid so.'

'Who would need to wedge the door?'

'Oh, the women doing the flowers on Saturday afternoon. They get water from the toilet off the vestry. Almost certainly one of them wedged it open and couldn't free it.'

Paul was getting flustered. 'I realize that I have been very remiss in not telling you this before but you can see that it has no special significance.'

'That is for me to judge. You neither saw nor heard anyone in the church, or in the vicinity, when you were going and returning?'

'I saw no-one.' He went on: 'I feel very guilty about this but, of course, I have never been in such a situation before. I was deeply shocked when I heard of Jessica's death and I suppose I was reluctant to involve myself.'

'The fact that your brother has now left, and that his whereabouts are unknown, has nothing to do with your belated decision to speak out?'

Paul's eyes widened. 'That is a most improper suggestion, Mr Wycliffe!'

'It was not a suggestion, it was a question, and when you withhold information from the police in a murder inquiry, it is the sort of question that is asked, and answers are sought. I would like to see the room which your brother occupied while he was here.'

'His room?' Paul seemed on the point of refusing but thought better of it. 'All right. If you will come with me . . .'

Wycliffe was taken to a large room at the back of the house on the first floor. It was a bedroom which had been turned into a bedsitter. Apart from the usual bedroom furniture, which included an unmade bed, there was a desk and, on the desk, a telephone and a rack of stationery. There was also a large ashtray holding a briar pipe. The lingering smell of pipe smoke rekindled a vague longing in Wycliffe.

Paul said: 'He's forgotten his pipe.'

'Nothing has been touched since he left this morning?'

'Everything is as he left it. As you see, even his bedding hasn't been removed.'

Wycliffe slid open the desk drawers; they were empty. On open shelves let into the alcove by the chimney breast there were several paperbacks. Wycliffe looked them over: the brainchildren of John le Carré, led by the inimitable Smiley.

'Are these his?'

'Yes, he has a taste for spy fiction.'

'I would like this room left as it is for the time being, Mr Paul. I'll send someone along to take a look at it.'

'Surely, Mr Wycliffe! . . . Are you implying that he might have a record?'

'You said yourself that his business activities were sometimes in a grey area of the law. From what the dead woman told her sister it is clear that she suspected him of some criminal involvement. She has been murdered, and I have to trace your brother if only to eliminate him from the inquiry.'

Paul was silenced.

'Just one more question, Mr Paul: when you saw her on Saturday evening, was she her usual self?'

The organist seemed dazed, but he made an effort. 'Entirely. She made some typical remark about flower arrangers who didn't know their own strength. I collected my music and when I left, she had already removed the wedge and she was polishing the tiles where it had scratched.'

'Thank you. Now, I must ask you to make a written statement concerning what you have told me. I suggest that you come to the Incident Room in the old school building some time this afternoon.'

Wycliffe left, thinking that it was one thing to take Arnold Paul down a peg or two, but quite another to imagine him or his elusive brother staging a melodramatic killing. But it was not impossible, and Philip or Timmy had made a quick and well-timed get-away.

Kersey crossed the square to the Trigg entrance. There was no gate, just two granite pillars with a much-weathered anonymous ornament on the top of each. Although it was not actually raining the air was saturated with moisture, and the moss, which grew on the gateposts and most of the stonework, was intensely green.

Three vehicles were parked on a freshly gravelled area near the house: a deluxe motor-caravan, a Rover saloon, and a Mini. The house had no particular shape, it seemed to have evolved at the whim of successive owners, all very long dead. The result was a pleasing jumble, mellowed by time, lichen, moss and ivy.

At any rate it pleased Kersey, who knew nothing of architecture but hated ostentation.

He had difficulty in finding the door, but when he did it was answered by a youngish woman, plump, pink, and freckled. 'Mrs Geach?'

'No. I suppose you're the policeman; you'd better go into the breakfast room.'

A room in which it was obvious that nobody ever had breakfast, it was a nondescript parking place for visitors who were not paying a social call.

Kersey sat for a couple of minutes gazing at gilt-framed furnishing landscapes, and an enormous walnut sideboard with a marble top on which there stood a hideously ornate samovar. Geach must have made a habit of collecting the left-overs from country-house sales.

Geach joined him, loose limbed, shambling, ready for anything.

'Mr Geach? . . . Inspector Kersey.'

'I was expecting your boss.'

'We all have our little disappointments, sir.'

Geach gave him a doubtful look and sat himself in one of the armchairs. Kersey was perched on one of the high-backed dining chairs with a leather seat.

'All right. Fire away.'

Kersey said, 'I can see you're not a man to beat about the bush; neither am I, so I'll get down to it. How well did you know your sister-in-law?'

Geach screwed up his lips. 'How well do you know yours? Assuming you've got one. She had the farm to run; my wife and I have our own lives; we didn't live in each other's pockets.'

'I saw the motor-caravan. Nice job.'

Geach became wary. 'So?'

'Handy for site work; handy too, I imagine, for entertaining the odd visitor in private.'

Geach remained cool. 'If you intend to be offensive, I should warn you—'

Kersey cut in with practised skill. 'No, I should warn you, Mr Geach, that this is a murder inquiry and, whatever you think, a lot of dirty linen will be fished out of the clothes basket. Whether it's all washed in public will depend on the people concerned. You, for instance; you can talk to me, man-to-man, or you can put up with us ferreting around for days, weeks – months if necessary. You don't need me to tell you that there aren't any real secrets in a place like this. Then, of course, there are the lads who work on your sites . . .'

Geach took a packet of mini cigars from his pocket and lit one. 'Smoke if you want to. Have one of these?'

'No, thanks, I'll smoke my own.'

Geach was looking at him with something like amusement. 'You're an impudent bastard, but I think we might get on.'

'Good! So you entertain the occasional woman in your van.' Kersey put on his best conspiratorial leer. 'Nothing to do with me unless one of 'em happens to have been Jessica Dobell. Think before you say anything, we've already had a hint along those lines and it wouldn't take much for us to have the forensic boys turn over the van.'

Geach drew deeply on his cigar and blew out a cloud of smoke. 'I don't believe this! I've got a bloody good mind to boot you out and put in a complaint.'

'It's up to you, sir, but I think we each had our reasons for coming to this little chat alone.'

Geach thought about this.

Kersey knew that he was on thin ice but he felt that he understood the contractor. He also understood why Wycliffe had given him the job instead of doing it himself.

Geach squinted at him through the smoke. 'All right; I don't suppose it will do me any harm unless you are a bigger fool than I take you for. Jessica did see the inside of my van a couple of times.'

'She was away from the farm three or four nights a month – two nights running a couple of times.'

'Not with me, she wasn't. Twice, as I said.' He seemed about to continue, but hesitated. Kersey, apparently indifferent, was looking out of the window watching Katherine, hands thrust deeply into the pockets of her mac, walking by the river. Geach went on: 'My sister-in-law, sex-ways, was a woman and a half, Inspector; damn nearly a nympho. She couldn't get enough.'

'You are saying there were others? The chap who lives there – Vinter, perhaps?'

'That's for sure, but she wouldn't want to be away nights for that, would she? All in working hours, so to speak.' Geach brushed ash from his jumper. 'No, the man you should be talking to is Lavin – the houseboat man – that's where she spent those nights away – some of 'em anyway. I intended to tell you that much before we started.'

'How do you know?'

'She told me.' He fixed Kersey with a quiet stare. 'She got some of her kicks that way – talking about it.' He shrugged. 'She pretended that in her book, sex-ways, I didn't rate very high; five out of ten, if that.' A crooked smile, 'While Lavin, if half of what she said was true, should have a medal to show for it. But I reckon that was her ploy, she probably did the same with him.' Geach became thoughtful. 'Jessica was one of those women who hates to take anything from a man. When she did, she couldn't bring herself to admit it.'

'You know Lavin?'

'I've only seen him a few times but he's lived in that boat for a couple of years – he took it over from Shorty Boase, when they put the old man into a home. Anyway, Lavin's very badly disfigured – doesn't show himself much; some sort of accident a few years back. But it didn't put Jessica off. No way.'

'Does he live by himself?'

Geach relit his cigar and spoke between rekindling puffs. 'No, he's got a boy living with him – I say boy, but he could be in his twenties. They call him Jumbo because he's a big chap and a bit ponderous. There's something odd about him, but he's Lavin's lifeline to the outside.'

Kersey was almost affable. 'Now, sir, if you can tell me the last occasion when the deceased visited your van . . .'

'It must have been early March, I could probably work it out.'

'You do that; ready for your statement.'

'You still want a statement?'

Kersey was cheerfully ironic. 'You must be joking! You've been sleeping with the victim of a sex killing and you ask me if we want a statement. You're in the target area, my friend, and I think you know it.' Kersey broke off and stood up. 'So let's say, this afternoon, at the old school, sir.'

Geach too, got to his feet. 'Will my wife have to know about Jessica?'

'Why should she? Unless it turns out you're the man we're looking for, then you'll have other things to worry about.'

'You're going to take a statement from her?'

'On the matter of what she was told by her sister about the situation between the Paul brothers. You don't have to worry. I'll send along a nice friendly DC and they can work it out between 'em here.'

As Geach followed him out into the hall a slim, dark girl flitted away down the passage.

'Your daughter?'

'Yes, damn it! Was that door shut?'

'Not quite.'

On the doorstep, Kersey said, 'What do you think of the Vinters?'

'Off the record?'

'Carried to the grave.'

'All right. Vinter's one of life's also-rans; two left feet. And Stephanie? She looks like a bit of Dresden china but there's a rumour Vinter isn't the boy's father.'

'What about the boy?'

Geach blew out his cheeks. 'He's supposed to be very bright but to my mind he's a poof in the making. Our Julie's got a thing about him and he's been to the house once or twice, but I told him to bugger off.'

Kersey left, pleased with himself; the contractor was no longer cocky.

Chapter Six

Easter Monday (continued)

'The dead woman's clothes, sir. Just returned from the path lab.'

Each item had been bagged and tagged separately: jeans, denim jacket, torn shirt, briefs, socks and slippers. Lucy Lane was laying them out on a trestle table in the Incident Room in case it became necessary to send them to Forensic.

Wycliffe was aware of a certain tension in her manner. 'What's the problem?'

'There's this; another anonymous.' She held out two polythene covers, one containing the envelope, the other the message.

'Another? Where did it come from?'

'It was found in the pocket of her jeans, sir. It's postmarked last Thursday, two days before she was killed.'

'Why wasn't it reported and dealt with last night?'

'It was missed when the body was stripped at the path lab. The clothes remained in the bins all night and the envelope was only found when they came to be bagged and logged this morning.'

Lucy waited for the obvious question: 'Who was attending?' But it didn't come. Wycliffe knew the virtue of the occasional blind eye. Somebody had boobed, but it wasn't the end of the world and nit-picking, to be effective, must be strictly rationed.

Lucy was still uneasy. 'Fox processed it this morning.'

Panic stations, obviously, and a closing of ranks. Lucy had been talked into being the sacrificial lamb; not in character. She went on, 'When it was found, the envelope hadn't been opened. It seems Jessica didn't attach much importance to these messages; she must have stuffed it into the pocket of her jeans and forgotten all about it.'

'What does it say?'

As with the others, the message was brief: 'These shall hate the whore and shall make her desolate and naked – Revelations 17:16.'

'What do you make of it?'

'It's different – an obvious threat this time.'

'The missing link in the chain?'

Lucy looked vague. 'I suppose it could be, sir, but the writing seems different as well as the aptness of the quotation – as though someone tried to imitate the others, not very successfully. The paper and envelope are the same as the others but anybody can buy them.' She added, abruptly, 'I would like to talk to the vicar's sister about these.'

'You think she sent them?'

'With respect, sir, it's only that she probably knows more of what goes on amongst the women of the village than anybody else – I mean, those connected with the church.'

'And you think a woman wrote these things?'

'I would like the chance to find out.' Lucy had recovered her poise. Obviously she thought the storm cones had been lowered.

'All right; go ahead. Anything else?'

'I had a word with DI Reed about the Ruses . . .' She added, to jog his memory: 'The cuttings in Jessica's photo album about the boy who was killed in the hit-and-run.'

'Well?'

'He remembers the case well. He was a sergeant in Traffic at the time and much involved. The lad was cycling home from Trispen at about half-six in the evening. It was winter, and dark, and he was hit by a motorist. His body and the bike were then pushed over the hedge, presumably to delay an inquiry, and not found until next morning. There were doubts as to whether the boy was dead when his body was pushed over, and local feeling was very strong.'

'The culprit was never found?'

'No. Johnny Glynn was a prime suspect but there was no evidence against him that would stand up in court. The inquiry went on for months and, in theory, the file is still open.'

Wycliffe had a vague recollection of reports concerning the investigation but he had not been directly involved. 'Ring DI Reed and say that I will look in on him tomorrow afternoon to discuss the case.'

It was mid-morning when Lucy arrived at the vicarage; the rain had stopped but it was still wet underfoot. The doorbell was answered by Celia, in person. Lucy introduced herself and showed her warrant card.

'My brother is in Truro for a meeting with the bishop.' Uncompromising. Lucy almost expected the door to be shut in her face.

'It was you I came to see – if you can spare me a few minutes.'

Celia Jordan was grey, her hair, her eyes, her skin, and her frock – the frock reminded Lucy of a nun's habit. And Celia's manner was bleak.

She hesitated, sizing up her visitor. 'All right, I can give you a few minutes. Wipe your feet – I've just hoovered the passage.'

The vicarage was modern, built by the Church Commissioners when they sold off their legacy of old and overlarge properties which catered for a more prosperous and fecund clergy. But the Jordans had contrived to give the place an appearance of being steeped in decades of ecclesiastical dreariness and gloom. There was an abundance of varnished woodwork, fawn and brown fabrics, and drab wallpapers relieved only by prints of holy pictures.

She was taken to a room at the back of the house, obviously the Vicar's study. There was a desk, a prie-dieu, and a great many shelves of religious works. It was dimly lit because the window was shielded by a conifer hedge grown close to the house. Celia occupied a swivel chair behind the desk and left Lucy with the choice of two kitchen chairs facing her. The reception of young people arranging weddings and christenings must have been equally grim.

Lucy presented the first three messages, arranging them on the desk. Her manner was ingratiating. 'You probably know the village and the villagers better than most. These are anonymous communications received by the dead woman in the weeks preceding her death and we are anxious to trace their source. I've really come to you for advice.'

Celia put on her spectacles which were secured by a silk cord about her neck. She studied the exhibits in silence. It was difficult to judge her age; her cheeks and forehead were smooth, but her mouth seemed slightly shrunken and her upper lip was corrugated with the finest wrinkles. Her examination of the exhibits was brief and when she looked up she seemed mildly impatient. 'You realize that these are quotations taken out of context? In their proper context they are largely metaphorical, even allegorical.'

Lucy was defensive. 'But they were copied out and sent

to the dead woman so, presumably, they were intended to apply to her.'

She received a bleak look over the top of the spectacles. 'That much is obvious. What more do you expect me to say?'

It was going to be hard going.

'You will know, of course, that Jessica's conduct was the subject of criticism by some in the village?'

'By me, you mean, and by women of the Guild. I make no apology for that; a woman with her reputation was quite unsuited to employment in the church. In this matter I disagreed with my brother.'

'So that you are to some extent in sympathy with the sender of these notes.'

A frown. 'They seem harmless. There can be no crime – certainly no sin, in reminding the wrongdoer of her error.'

'As they stand, they seem rather pointless. What could they be expected to achieve?'

Celia removed her spectacles and chose to be sententious: 'One should never underestimate the power of the word.'

'But a threat might have made it more effective.'

'I see no threat in these at any rate.'

Lucy produced the fourth message and handed it over. 'This was sent two days before Jessica was murdered.'

The glasses were replaced and this time the examination took longer. She brought out a Bible from one of the desk drawers and referred to it briefly.

The woman was obviously intelligent and she had a formidable presence. Lucy was reminded of a university tutor under whom she had suffered; a female dragon who commonly handed out the look she now received, usually with a barbed comment: 'Your essay displays a singular, one might say a perverted, talent for missing the obvious.'

Celia contented herself with: 'Surely you must see that

this fourth specimen comes from a different source?'

'What makes you say so?'

'Whoever sent the first three, knew her Bible. She may have used a concordance, but she knew how to use it effectively.' Celia held up her hand when Lucy would have spoken. 'Yes, yes! All right! I said "her", and "she", and that is what I meant. These are the work of a woman; there can be no doubt of that.

'Anyway, my second point is that the first three quotations are both accurate and apt, whereas the fourth is neither. A sentence has been made by inserting a capital letter where there was none, and the context is not only allegorical but ludicrously inept.' She was contemptuous.

She went on, her manner accusing, 'I don't know if you have looked up the source paragraph?' And she quoted, giving Lucy no chance to reply: '"And the ten horns which thou sawest on the beast, these shall hate the whore and shall make her desolate and naked."'

A faint smile. 'One would have to be very much at sea before making use of such a source when there are so many more apt ones to choose from.'

Lucy said, meekly, 'That thought had occurred to me.'

'Really.' Celia was not interested; she was shuffling the exhibits, comparing them. 'Apart from that it seems clear that the fourth envelope and message were written by a different hand. However, that is not my concern.' She gathered the polythene wrappers together and handed them back. 'Now, if that is all . . . ?'

Lucy had only a vague idea of what she expected from her interview with the vicar's sister but this was certainly not it. She felt more than ever like a first-year student being dismissed after a tutorial that had gone badly wrong. On the other hand, the woman had confirmed her own ideas about the fourth message, and she had an argument to put to Wycliffe.

* * *

Much of Wycliffe's time during any case was taken up with what he called 'fringe activites' – extended telephone conversations with the chief, and with his own deputy, back at headquarters; receiving and reacting to reports concerning other cases all over the two counties, in fact, with the CID management of the police area as a whole. He was fortunate in that his deputy preferred administration to work on the ground – a case of Jack Spratt would eat no fat and his wife would eat no lean. So it worked, and made it possible for him to commit himself to individual investigations of importance.

But, like any other, the present case had its share of administrative and public relations chores. Even on this Easter Monday morning, Bertram Oldroyd, his chief, wanted to know what was going on; and, more remarkable still, the media were turning up in force for a briefing.

Oldroyd was relaxed and teasing. 'You attract these headline-grabbing cases, Charles. Sometimes I think you work it with the media. Seriously, though, is this a piece of black magic ghoulishness or has it been dressed up to look like one?'

Wycliffe, as always on such occasions, aimed to be both brief and vague. 'I don't know . . . I doubt if it's a cult thing.'

'What, then?'

He resented being forced to condense his vaporous notions and impressions into words which, once spoken, condition one's later thoughts. 'I feel that there is hatred behind this thing, and not only against the murdered woman.'

'You think there could be other killings?'

He said, with a curtness and finality, hardly diplomatic in speaking to the chief, 'I've no idea.'

'If you think we are dealing with some kind of psychopath . . .'

'I don't have any view on that at the moment, sir.'

And the telephone was dropped at the other end, with Oldroyd saying to himself, 'One of these days . . .'

In fact, Oldroyd's questions were little different from those he could expect from the reporters when they arrived.

The media is not easily roused from its weekend lethargy. Even in a normal week an investigation which starts on a Sunday stands some chance of escaping serious attention until halfway through Monday. Then their interest depends on certain 'newsworthy' features. As Wycliffe feared, this one had them all, and when the time arrived for the briefing he faced a whole gaggle of reporters and a couple of TV cameras. The murder of Jessica Dobell was news.

But they were good humoured. 'You don't need my help to embroider this one, it's ready made.' They knew him of old and there was an element of camaraderie. At least three of the older men had worked his patch for twenty years. To give them something he dropped a word about the anonymous notes.

'What did they say, these notes?'

'They were quotations from the Bible. I'm not prepared to quote them at the moment.'

'The Bible can be pretty gruesome. Were they abusive? Threatening?'

'Cautionary, I'd say.'

'Were they sent by the killer?'

'As I don't know the killer or who sent the notes that's a difficult question.'

After ten minutes or so they sheared off to the pub. A few drinks, a scout round the village, a spot of chatting-up the locals, and that would be that for a while.

Back in the office he was joined by Kersey, reporting on the Geach interview. Kersey summed up: 'Geach is no fool and he has his eye to the main chance. It's hard to say whether he would have the knowledge or the inclination to rig the set-up in the church, but if it served his purpose he might be capable of anything.'

Kersey yawned. 'It's obvious he thinks he's in the frame and I encouraged him to go on thinking that way. Incidentally, he's more amenable than he might be because he doesn't want his wife to know he'd been sleeping with her sister.'

Kersey yawned again, this time with total abandon. 'This place makes me sleepy – enervating they call it. Anyway, most of what Geach said is in his statement; what isn't, is in my report. Mainly he was anxious to divert attention from himself, and he chose the houseboat man – Lavin. According to him Lavin had been having it off with the girl on a regular basis.'

Wycliffe turned the pages of his copy of the file. 'Have we got anything on this Lavin, apart from Geach's story?'

Kersey said, 'He crops up in the reports. He bought the houseboat just over two years ago and went there to live with his friend – or whatever the boy is. It seems Lavin is a biochemist; he worked for one of the big drug firms until he was badly injured in a gas explosion. According to gossip he got hefty compensation.'

'Any idea how he spends his time now?'

'He's taken up natural history and he's supposed to be making a study of life in the creeks and streams about here. The boy goes off in a canoe, collecting samples and they say the boat is like a laboratory.'

'So we need to know more about him.' Wycliffe looked up at the clock. 'But it can wait until after lunch.'

They had a snack meal at one of the bar tables where there were too many near neighbours to talk shop, so there was little said. Wycliffe watched a couple at the next table, a man and a young girl who, between mouthfuls of cottage pie, jointly attacked *The Times*' crossword. The man's auburn hair, silvery at the ends, hung to his shoulders and his untrimmed beard reached to his chest. Yet his face, where it could be seen, had a youthful freshness. Wycliffe was reminded of storybook pictures of Rip Van Winkle. The girl, fair, with an English rose complexion, had that demure composure of a young lady from a Victorian drawing room.

Wycliffe was intrigued; they spoke little, there were murmurs and small gestures, and from time to time one of them would pick up the pencil and make an entry on the grid, all with an air of felicity and of total contentment in each other's company.

As he was leaving, Wycliffe had a quiet word with Johnny, the landlord.

Johnny said, 'Hector St John Carey and his niece, Alicia.'

'They come here often?'

'Almost every day.'

Wycliffe remembered the riverside house with a folly like a lighthouse. 'The house with the folly?'

'Trecara, the house with the folly.'

Wycliffe was puzzled by the abrupt change in the landlord's attitude whenever he was asked about someone living in the village. In his professional role he was amiable, even chatty; but a question about any of the villagers brought down the closed sign. His replies became taciturn, his manner suspicious.

When Wycliffe and Kersey returned to the Incident Room, each to his own report, Wycliffe was interrupted by a phone call from Franks, the pathologist.

'Nothing new, old chap! Healthy woman. Fit. Muscles like a navvy; I wouldn't care to have tangled with her except in a friendly.'

'Not pregnant by any chance?'

'Nor by any mischance, though you won't be surprised to learn that she was no virgin. She died, in case you're still interested, as a result of a massive depressed fracture of the skull involving the temporal bone of the left side.'

Wycliffe said, 'Don't tell me, I know: the blow was probably inflicted with a blunt instrument such as a hammer. Thanks.'

Franks chuckled. 'We do our best, but we can't solve all your cases for you, Charles.'

Wycliffe had no sooner dropped the telephone than Fox arrived with his report. Fox's reports were models of their kind: scale diagrams, meticulously drawn, and enlarged photographs, all interspersed with Fox's idiosyncratic prose in pristine type. The man worked like a mole and Wycliffe was expected, not unreasonably, to show appreciation. Having done so, he looked at the formidable wad of paper and asked, 'Anything for special attention?'

'There's the toeprint, sir.' He turned the pages to a blow-up, contrast-intensified, of the mud flake print found on the carpet in the aisle of the church. 'It's from the toe of a left rubber boot, sir. An acquaintance in the trade says it's almost certainly size nine or ten and it might just be possible to identify the boot if we find it.

'At any rate we know that the dead woman wore rubber boots and they are missing but they were fives.'

Wycliffe should have been interested, and tried to sound so. 'It's worth following up. Anything else?'

'The pieces of paper used to wedge the organ keys came from the *Church Quarterly* for September of last year. There are quite good prints on two of the pieces, unidentified at the moment. It's a theological publication and, according to the newsagent, it is ordered specially for the vicar.'

'Good! So that narrows the field. No luck with any of the other prints?'

'Not so far, sir.'

Wycliffe picked up his ballpoint and tried to look politely dismissive. Reluctantly, Fox took the hint and left.

The truth is that whatever the contributions from technical and forensic boffins, the hard core of police investigation still consists in what people can be persuaded to tell them. And persuasion becomes increasingly difficult as the champions of everybody's liberty but the victim's turn the thing into a chess game.

Wycliffe pushed Fox's papers away, sighed, and returned to his work. Ten minutes later when he was settling once more to the business of digesting facts and regurgitating them in the bland porridge of a report, he was interrupted again by a tap at the door: Dixon with a letter.

'Sent on by messenger from the Truro nick, sir.'

The envelope was addressed in a woman's hand, schoolgirl style, to: 'Superintendent Wycliffe, Truro Police Station.' The single sheet it contained was headed: 'Tilly's Cottage, Bell Hill, Moresk, Nr Truro.' The message was brief:

> Dear Mr Wycliffe,
> I can't come to see you but if you come here I might be able to help you. I am at home after six o'clock each evening. It is no good sending someone else and you must treat this as confidential.
> Yours sincerely,
> Grace Trevena (Miss)

Every case entices its ration of nutters out of the woodwork. They write letters, usually anonymous, make phone calls, often in funny voices, and even volunteer fictitious statements. This was probably a sample, but there was something about it, a certain basic simplicity, which struck him as unusual. And Trevena was a good Cornish name. He picked up his telephone.

'Is PC Trice there? . . . Send him in, please.'

Trice was the local Community Policeman, now seconded for duty with the squad. He came in, uneasily diffident. 'Sir?'

'Tilly's Cottage – know where it is?'

A look of relief. 'At the top of Bell Hill where it joins Church Lane, sir.'

'And Grace Trevena, who lives there?'

A slow smile. 'I know her; a youngish woman, probably middle-thirties, lives with her grandmother. She's hooked on astrology and fortune-telling . . . She runs a little shop in the market selling the gear and she writes bits for the local papers, "Your Stars this Week", sort of thing. There's also a society . . . Perhaps she's a bit loony but she's pleasant enough.'

'Thanks; that's what I wanted to know.'

As the door closed behind Trice he added to himself, 'Easier to buy a Ouija board.'

'Disraeli B. *Whigs and Whiggism. Political Writings*. Edited by W. Hutcheon 1913.' Stephanie Vinter stood on the library steps against a section of shelves, the book in her hands. 'Hutcheon is spelt: H-U-T-C-H-E-O-N.'

Seated at the long table, Giles entered the book on a numbered, ruled sheet, while, on the other side of the room, Hector St John Carey stood on another set of steps and called down to his niece, Alicia: 'Halliway J. O. *Rambles in Western Cornwall*. First edition 1861.'

The room, with its barrel roof, had some resemblance to the nave of a church, and there were mullioned Gothic windows at each end, but the walls were lined with bookcases which reached to the springing of the roof.

'I've brought you some tea.' A lean, grey-haired woman with a croaking voice arrived with a tray.

Carey descended the steps and took the tray from her. 'That is very kind of you, Winnie. So thoughtful . . .'

Perhaps books, even on shelves, have a civilizing influence. What sort of deviant feels belligerent in a library?

The four of them gathered at the table. Stephanie poured; Carey passed the biscuits, murmuring pleasant nothings into his beard. They cooed at each other like doves. Then Carey said, 'It's good of you to help us, Giles; I hope that you are not bored. This paperwork is not very stimulating but they tell me that if you have a library, then you must have a catalogue. I don't know precisely why this is, but I am quite sure that your mother could tell you.'

Giles flushed, pushed up his glasses and smiled.

Stephanie thought, how long is it since I've seen him smile?

Alicia, wearing a grey overall, looked supremely beautiful.

Carey went on, 'What could be nicer than tea in the library with an intelligent young man and two women who are beautiful as well as intelligent?'

When second cups had been poured, Carey ventured, 'Are there any developments at the farm?'

Stephanie patted her lips with a handkerchief. 'Laurence is expecting to hear from their solicitor. That, I suppose, will be the end.'

Carey stroked the silkiness of his beard. 'You know that I meant what I said? Nothing would give me greater pleasure than to share this place with you – such as it is. You may wish to come for a time – until some other arrangements are made, or you may favour living with us permanently. Alicia and I lead a rather lonely existence, cut off as we are, and it would be good for both of us to have congenial companions. Is that not so, Alicia?'

'You know that I agree, Uncle.'

'There now!' He reached for another biscuit. 'These are good. Winnie makes them herself . . .' When he had bitten into the biscuit he went on: 'Do you know the meaning of Trecara in Cornish? It means the homestead of Cara and the word cara translates as friend.' He added, his eyes mischievous: 'Or even as love and, of course, Carey comes from the same root.'

Stephanie said, 'You are more than kind, Hector, but Laurence would find it difficult to accept such one-sided hospitality.'

Carey spread his hands. 'I do not see it as one-sided, but talk it over. I think that it would be a good arrangement for all of us.'

Giles looked at his mother. 'Is Mr Carey suggesting that we might come here to live?'

Carey said, 'Does the idea distress you, Giles?'

Giles flushed but did not reply.

On the houseboat not far away a man sat reading. The light fell upon the right side of his head and face, on his sandy hair and beard, in both of which there were streaks of grey. His features were lean and the prominent bone structure was hardly masked at all by the pointed beard. The gross disfigurement on the left side was softened by shadows but the pale scar tissue was evident even to the casual eye.

The boy sat at a bench, looking down a binocular microscope; the beam of the lamp was directed through the mirror on to a tiny watch-glass placed on the stage. The boy was massively built; he had a large head, dark hair, cut short, and a round face, amiable in its immaturity.

'The little beggar won't keep still.'

The man looked up from his book. 'Try adding a drop of glycerine.'

Incredibly, the great hand with its thick fingers performed the delicate operation of sucking up a little glycerine from a bottle into a pipette and adding one drop to the water in the watch-glass.

There was a smile on the smooth features. 'Ah, that's better; he's not so lively now. He looks like some sort of larva . . .'

'Is the body divided into segments?'

'Oh, yes.'

'Can you see a head?'

'Yes, he has a head—'

'And the rest of the body in two parts?'

'Yes—'

'Any legs?'

The boy peered down the microscope. 'Yes, he's got six legs on the middle – on the thorax.' He brought out the word with evident pleasure.

'So it's an . . .'

'An insect – I ought to have bin able to work that out, didn't I?'

'You need practice, that's all. Now let's see if you can decide whether it's a larva, a nymph, or an adult . . .'

The exchange continued to a resolution of the problem and the man returned to his reading. It was high tide and the houseboat was afloat so that there were creaks and chuckles to disturb the stillness. Once a duck squawked in fright and somewhere, distantly, a dog barked.

The boy said, 'Nice, isn't it?'

'What's nice?'

'Well, being on our own again. She's not going to come in and spoil it.'

'Shut up, Jumbo!'

The man's voice was peremptory, angry, and the boy's

features seemed to crumple. 'I'm sorry, Brian . . . Really I didn't mean to . . . I just thought . . .'

'Yes, I know. Don't get upset. But you mustn't talk like that.' He added after a pause, 'Play me something, Jumbo.'

'Shall I?'

'Please.'

The boy fetched an accordion from under a bench seat and, after a preliminary trial, started to play. It was a strange melody which seemed always on the point of repetition, of finding a theme, then losing it in a fresh adventure. The man discarded his book and sat back in his chair, eyes closed; the boy's face became serious and intent. After a few minutes he stopped playing and put the accordion aside.

'Time for supper.'

The man said: 'You're right, Jumbo . . . It is nice.'

Chapter Seven

Easter Monday evening

The triumvirate assembled in Wycliffe's little office. Kersey lit a cigarette and, ostentatiously, Lucy Lane threw open the window to the dusk outside. Wycliffe looked from one to the other but made no comment.

'It's time to look at what we've got.'

Each of them had a file containing copies of the reports and statements so far. Idly, they turned the pages, searching for inspiration which failed to come. Wycliffe, at his most dry and succinct, gave an account of his interview with Arnold Paul.

'You've got a copy of his statement and you'll see it puts him in the crosswires as far as means and opportunity are concerned. As to motive, it could be that Jessica really did stumble on something that would have put him and/or his brother on the spot. CRO have nothing on either of them. So, if the brother is bent, he's been lucky, or he's worked under another name.'

Kersey said, 'Perhaps they're not brothers.'

Wycliffe agreed. 'Which would implicate Arnold. I had a word with Geoff Cox of the Met Fraud Squad. He'd never heard of Philip but he knew Arnold and his bank – nothing against either, but he promised to ask around and get what he can in the way of background. Meantime, I arranged for Fox to go over the man's room and he's sent off a set of prints to CRO just in case.'

He turned to Kersey. 'What about the other statements? I haven't read them.'

Kersey grimaced. 'As bland as milk. When you read them you begin to think that there never was a woman lying there in the church with her head bashed in.'

'I believe you've got a line on the Vinter breakdown.'

Kersey said: 'Yes, he's got no form but the word breakdown is a euphemism for getting the sack. He was suspended in eighty-five for sexually assaulting a girl student. I got this from a mate of mine in Bristol CID. He knew about it because there was a police investigation but no prosecution. It was more than a bit iffy and Vinter was allowed to resign. The girl was no Persil-white virgin and the feeling was that Vinter misread her signals or that she was working off a grudge.'

Lucy Lane, turning the pages of her file, said, 'He would be an expert at misreading signals where women are concerned.'

Kersey shrugged. 'You would know about that. At any rate, it cost the poor bastard his job.'

Wycliffe cut in: 'None of which disqualifies Vinter as a suspect, so we need to keep an eye on him. All right. We already know about Geach, so it's over to you, Lucy – your interview with the vicar's sister – Celia, isn't it?'

Wycliffe looked bored. He saw this as a routine exchange of information to save everybody having to wade through the reports. At these sessions he discouraged discussion. More than once he had been known to say, 'There are times when listening to other people's ideas only confuses my own.' An attitude which was more defensive than bigoted.

Lucy Lane summarized her visit to the vicarage. 'Celia is a very intelligent woman, but there's something odd about her.' She hesitated, then plunged. 'I think she sent the first three notes herself.'

'Did you put it to her?'

Lucy, to Wycliffe's surprise, flushed; an unusual phenomenon. 'No, sir. She is a very formidable woman. If it comes to a confrontation I would want to be better prepared. I wouldn't want to start something I couldn't finish.'

Kersey looked at her in mock amazement. 'This woman I must see!'

Wycliffe let it pass. 'So, at least, you don't think she was responsible for the fourth note?'

'No. That took her by surprise. And, as you know, I'm not happy about that fourth note. I would like to have all four submitted for expert opinion.'

'Why not? We must also get something on the Jordans' background. Let's know who we are dealing with. Anything else?'

For a few minutes conversation drifted away from the case. Wycliffe and Kersey speculated, dismally, about the probable findings of the Criminal Justice Commission while Lucy continued to study her file.

Finally Wycliffe sat back in his chair, stretched, yawned, and looked at the clock. 'Well, nobody will listen to us; that's for sure. It's time for our meal . . . Lucy! Aren't you eating this evening?'

Lucy was still absorbed in her file. 'I was looking at his signature on my xerox of his statement.'

'Who are you talking about?'

'Geach.' Lucy pushed the open file across the desk and both men examined it. Wycliffe said, 'A bit florid.'

Kersey shrugged. 'Takes up a lot of paper, but so what? Chaps like Abe Geach boost their ego with a flashy signature.'

Lucy said: 'He signs himself Abe G Geach, but the last four letters are no more than a scrawl.'

Wycliffe was impatient. 'Come on, Lucy, if you've got

anything, let's have it. My signature ends in a scrawl too.'

'No comment, sir. But just read aloud the letters that are legible.'

Wycliffe muttered as though to himself, 'ABEGG . . . Well, I'm damned!'

'It must be chance,' said Kersey.

'It's certainly odd,' Wycliffe replied. 'But could there possibly be a connection?'

Lucy Lane said, 'I can't believe that it's chance.'

Wycliffe was studying the signature. 'Neither can I. Which means that whoever wedged the organ keys did it to draw attention to Geach.'

Kersey said, 'This is better thought about after a good meal.'

In contrast with the night before, several of the tables in the restaurant were empty and others were occupied by couples and threesomes there for a quiet meal. Wycliffe's table, in a corner by one of the windows, was a little removed from the others, a testimony to the discretion of the landlord.

The man himself came to take their order. 'Only one main dish tonight – *coq au vin*. It's the real thing – none of your boiled chicken warmed up in a prepared sauce but, if you don't fancy it, I can do you ham-off-the-bone with a decent salad.'

Coq au vin was agreed.

'I can offer you a red burgundy which goes very well.'

Kersey said, 'I'm beginning to like this place.'

They had reached the dessert stage before the case was mentioned and it was Kersey who said, 'It strikes me as bloody silly whichever way you look at it. I mean, if Geach did the killing he'd hardly put his signature to it – musical or otherwise, and, surely, the same argument would stop anybody else with an ounce of common sense from trying to incriminate him in that way.'

Lucy Lane, meticulously dissecting a pear, said, 'I suppose the fact that the organ was used draws attention to Paul as the organist—'

Wycliffe cut in, 'Full marks, Lucy, for spotting the signature business but it adds one more bizarre feature to this case which bristles with them already. Instead of looking for runners in the means, motive and opportunity stakes, we might try to work out the kind of person who could lay on such an exhibition.' Wycliffe picked up his coffee cup and put it down again. 'Think of it: after the woman was killed by a blow to the head, her body was dragged to the statue of Christ so that her hair could be draped over the sandalled feet . . . Either then, or before, she was undressed to the precise extent which would suggest obscenity without implying a sexual assault in the ordinary sense.'

Kersey was about to say something but Wycliffe stopped him. 'No, Doug, let me finish. After all that, he or she goes to the organ and wedges the appropriate keys, apparently to suggest Geach's involvement through his shared initials with the Schumann Variations, as well as a musical connection. Add to this that the bits of folded paper were carefully cut from a religious magazine, subscribed to by the vicar, and the whole seems to suggest a deliberate plan to involve, if not incriminate, several people.'

Wycliffe paused just long enough to sip his coffee, which had gone cold. 'Having laid on his charade, the killer then starts up the blower on the organ and simply walks away.'

He frowned in a final effort to give his ideas coherence. 'It's been my impression from the first that this tableau, or whatever one calls it, was intended to make a point beyond the death of Jessica Dobell. Now, of course, aside from all this, we have these anonymous notes which may or may not be the work of the killer but must be fitted into the pattern.'

He drank off the remainder of his coffee, made a wry face, and patted his lips with his table napkin. 'Let's think all this over and see if we can get some sort of notion of the kind of man or woman we are looking for – without trying to fit any particular individual into the frame.'

He looked at his watch. 'But not tonight. Tonight I'm having my walk.'

He set out to explore the village beyond the square and found himself in a pattern of three or four short streets made up, for the most part, of terraced houses with their front doors opening on to the pavement. There were shops, a Methodist chapel big enough to accommodate the whole population, and a pub. This was a fresh aspect of the village and it was where most of the villagers lived.

There was still light in the sky but curtains were drawn across many windows and fragments of TV programmes filtered through. From the pub came the murmur of voices and an occasional burst of laughter but over most of the village there was silence and the streets were deserted. It was half past eight.

These evening walks over the ground where he happened to be working were necessary to him, especially in small towns and rural communities. He had to get the 'feel' of the place, to have some idea of what it was like to live there. To start with he was an intruder, perhaps a threat. Sometimes he felt heir to the witch doctor, prowling at night among the huts of the villagers, peeking, prying and eavesdropping.

The notion appealed to him. Perhaps in the morning he should line up his suspects, place a dry pebble in the mouth of each, and woe betide the one whose pebble stayed dry. (Add that one to his training school lectures on Modern Investigatory Procedures.)

A steepish hill was lined with more little houses, but these were stepped against the slope. An enamelled blue and white sign on the corner house read 'Bell Hill'. He remembered that the woman who wrote to him, the fortune-teller, or whatever she was, lived at the top of Bell Hill, at the junction with Church Lane . . . Grace Trevena, that was it!

As he climbed the hill he found that he had decided to call on her. From witch doctors to fortune-tellers by easy stages. King Saul visited the Witch of Endor by night and modern police chiefs had been known to enlist diviners to find their missing bodies. Whimsical thoughts of the head of CID on his evening stroll. Did other apparently responsible and sage officials have such rag-bag minds? Sometimes it troubled him that the persona he presented to the world was such a fake.

Tilly's Cottage belonged neither to the rather dreary little terraced houses of Bell Hill, nor to the grander villas of Church Lane. Placed on a corner between the two it was a solid little house in its own garden, surrounded by pine trees. There was a light in one of the downstairs rooms.

Wycliffe opened the gate and walked down the crazy-paving path to the front door. His ring was answered by a female voice. 'Who is it, please?'

'Superintendent Wycliffe.'

He had envisaged a stringy female, close to forty, casting about for a tolerable route across the sterile plane of virginity. Instead he was confronted by a plump young woman with a mass of dark curls and a friendly grin.

'I'm Grace Trevena. So you've come. I've been wondering whether you would and thought you probably wouldn't.'

He was shown into a homely, comfortable living room

turned almost into a jungle by potted plants. An elderly woman sat knitting by an electric fire and, on the dining table, there was a portable typewriter, a few books with places marked, a box of paper and some carbons.

'This is my grandmother, who brought me up.'

The old lady acknowledged him with becoming formality.

Grace said: 'Will you have a drink? Sherry or gin – that's our limit, I'm afraid.'

He refused a drink but accepted a chair, and the girl resumed her seat at the table but turned to face him.

'I'm in the middle of my weekly article. I expect you've been told that I'm interested in the occult and that sort of thing. I've not got what it takes to do research but I learn from people who have and try to apply their methods. We have a society, and I run a little stall in Truro market where I sell the literature, cards, charts, and so on.'

She smiled as she spoke, so that one had the impression that it was all good fun. 'I'm telling you all this because it was how I came to meet Jessica in the first place.'

Wycliffe listened politely, the old lady's needles continued to click, and Grace never stopped talking.

'You don't look comfortable to me. Stretch out your legs and rest your head back. Make yourself at home. As I was saying, Jessica came to me for a Tarot reading and we ended up by doing a series.'

The plump girl's face was suddenly serious. 'It was worrying. I've never known such a series, so consistent, and so – well, threatening.'

'What was threatened?'

'Oh, her death – and death by violence. Of course I didn't let on to her. I mean, one can't. You do see that, don't you? I interpreted it as a crisis in her life but I was never in much doubt as to the nature of the crisis – if my reading was anything like right.'

'When did she first come to see you?'

'When was it, Gran? Seven – eight months ago?'

'It was last September, when we had the first decent weather of the year.'

She went on: 'I don't expect you to believe all this stuff about the Tarot and so on. I mean, you're not a convert, but I mention it because it led to us becoming quite friendly. Jessica confided in me. People do. When you take up this sort of work you get to be something like a priest – I mean, people rely on you to keep their secrets because it's your sort of profession . . .'

'Jessica told you things about her life?'

'Yes, she did, and I feel, now that she's gone, I'm free to talk if it would help to find out who killed her.'

'What did she tell you?'

'Oh, about the farm, about the Vinters, and about her affairs with men. She had quite a sense of humour when she got going. Of course, she was Aries – fairly typical – energetic, belligerent, and highly sexed . . . But not all that sure of herself underneath. I mean, she worried, and she had a sense of guilt which many Aries subjects don't . . . What are you, by the way? I'd put you down as a Leo.'

Wycliffe felt trapped, mesmerized. 'I was born on August the fifteenth.'

'There you are then! Fortunately you don't have the aggressiveness which sometimes goes with the Leo make-up. But as you get older, watch out for back trouble. Could be heart, but I don't think so.'

'You were telling me about Jessica.'

'Yes, I was. I can't keep to the point, can I? I'm a true Piscean – never know where I'm going until I'm coming back. Well, one evening last week she came here – Good Friday, it was, and I could see that she was worried and depressed. Even Arians have their fits of depression.'

Wycliffe, on the verge of losing patience, asked, 'What was she worried about?'

'Well, she started by asking if I'd seen in the local paper that Mrs Ruse, over to Tresillian, was dead. She reminded me that this was the mother . . .'

'Of the boy killed in a hit-and-run several years ago.'

She looked at him in surprise. 'So you know about that! Well, they never found out who did it and Jessica said that she knew who was responsible and that she had been involved. She'd been trying to put it out of her mind ever since, but with the mother dying, and people saying the poor woman had never got over her grief – well, it brought it all back as bad as ever.'

'She said that she was actually involved in the accident?'

'That was how I understood her.'

'Did she say who was with her?'

Grace looked embarrassed. 'No. I asked her if it was Johnny Glynn – I shouldn't have done, I know, I was just being inquisitive. But with all the rumours . . . Anyway, she said it wasn't Johnny; that he'd told the truth. She asked me if I thought this was the crisis the Tarot predicted and I was weak; I said it might be.'

'And?'

The fat girl looked down at her hands. 'She seemed very upset and said she supposed she'd have to go to the police. Then there was a bit about not having played fair with her sister and not wanting to make it worse. I didn't quite understand that.' She looked at Wycliffe, soft eyed. 'I wasn't much help to her, was I? She left more worried than she came. Then, the very next night . . .'

Wycliffe said nothing and she went on, 'I didn't know whether to tell you all this. I mean, I don't really know anything and I could easily get somebody into trouble. I decided to leave it to fate; I usually find that's the best way.' She looked at him, earnestly searching for approval. 'I wrote to you and gave you the option. If you didn't come to see me, well that would be that. If you did, it wouldn't have been my decision.'

Wycliffe leaned forward in his chair. 'Miss Trevena . . .'

'Call me Grace, please. Everybody does.'

'All right, Grace – you do realize that Jessica was murdered and that her murderer has not been caught. He or she could kill again. What I am saying is that anything you can tell me of her life could be important. You spoke of the men with whom she had affairs. Who were they?'

The girl's voice was low. 'She mentioned Mr Geach – I suppose that's why she felt guilty about her sister; then there was the man on the houseboat, and Mr Vinter.'

'No-one else?'

'No, I don't think so.'

Wycliffe became stern. 'Look at me, Grace!'

The brown eyes were solemn but not scared. The old lady's needles ceased to click.

'Think now, Grace! Was there anything else that Jessica told you about anyone – anyone at all, that reflected on them in a mean or discreditable way; anything they would not want to be known? If you tell me things that turn out to have no relevance then they will never be mentioned again, I can promise you that.'

The girl's brow wrinkled. 'I can't think of anything really . . .'

'But?'

'Well, it was quite a while ago now, just before Christmas. Jess was laughing about it.'

'About what?'

'Well, it seems so mean to tell you, but if I must . . . Jessica went to the church one morning, to get things ready for a christening in the afternoon, and when she opened the vestry door, the vicar was there with the Vinter boy. He was hugging the boy – fondling his hair. That was all . . . I mean, there was nothing dirty going on . . . But Jessica reckoned the vicar was a bit that way.'

'All the same, you were quite right to tell me.'

Unexpectedly, the old lady joined in. 'What Grace does with her cards and all that stuff is her business; it's nothing to do with me; I don't interfere. But I didn't like that Dobell woman in my house. There was something about her. I'm sorry she's been murdered but she's the sort of woman, in my opinion, who asked for it.'

A faint smile reappeared on the face of the fat girl. 'Now you know what Gran thinks.'

She saw him out, and he walked down Church Lane and back to the pub, thoughtful. The Hopton was quiet, the restaurant was closed and only a few regulars lingered about the bar.

'A nightcap, Mr Wycliffe?'

'No. No, thank you.' He was in no mood for Johnny. From the telephone in the passage upstairs he said 'Good night' to Helen.

In bed, with the light out, he lay staring through the open window at a rectangle of starlit sky. He listened to the few late drinkers being seen off the premises, the muttered partings, the footsteps; then Johnny locking up. There must be a private part of the house, for he did not hear Johnny climbing the stairs. In fact the silence was so complete that he found himself listening to it as though to something positive.

A lot had happened in this first full day. It seemed a long time since Lucy's kedgeree. But were they any further forward? He had been right about Jessica; there was a history of trauma which could explain her frenzied life style. The Ruse boy: she had admitted to some part in his death. But through action or by association? Was it guilt or guilty knowledge? Either way, could it have any significance as a motive for her murder? Vendettas reaching out across the years are material for fiction, but they are rare in fact.

In the matter of suspects and evidence: no material progress; just a lucky dip. Were there any suspects with a credible motive? The Vinters? Certainly there was bitterness, possibly hatred. But murder? What did they gain? Geach – to divert attention from himself had brought in Lavin, the houseboat man. At most it was a banal little tale of sex which must be kept from the wife – for her own good, of course. Still, he must talk to Lavin.

Wycliffe sighed, and turned on his side. He thought of Arnold Paul and his precious brother. He felt in his bones that despite appearances they were a sideshow. And the vicar? It was possible that the vicar was homosexually inclined, and not impossible that Jessica had used the fact against him. But murder? And in his own church?

Wycliffe decided that he had had enough. He thumped his pillow, made a convulsive turn, and to his own surprise, felt suddenly relaxed.

Chapter Eight

Tuesday

At seven o'clock on Tuesday morning, almost forty-eight hours after Jessica Dobell was found dead on the chancel steps, Michael Jordan and his sister, Celia, were at breakfast. Even at breakfast Michael was already wearing his clerical collar and vest. Celia's grey eyes regarded her brother across the table with diagnostic rather than sympathetic concern.

'You are looking ill, Michael.'

The vicar paused, a spoonful of All-bran halfway to his lips. 'The last two days have been a strain. I suppose it shows.' His manner was defensive.

'I warned you about that woman, Michael. She was not a fit person to have in the church.'

The vicar parried with a professional response. 'The church is for sinners, Celia.'

'For sinners who repent. That woman was blatant in her sin and you allowed her to profit from the church.'

'She profited very little, poor soul; she worked hard for what she got.'

Celia continued to stare at her brother as though by concentration she might read his mind, and he flushed under her silent scrutiny. She said, at last, 'I don't think you've told me everything, Michael.'

'What more could there be to tell?'

Celia sipped her coffee without taking her eyes off him.

'I've been thinking: you went across to the church on Saturday evening – at around eight it must have been.'

'I went to fetch my new service book.'

'So you said. Was the Dobell woman there then?'

Michael's flush deepened. 'Yes.'

'You didn't mention it at the time.'

'Would you expect me to? You know quite well that Jessica was often there of an evening, especially if there was a service the following day.'

'Perhaps that is why you found these evening visits so necessary.'

'Celia! What are you suggesting?' She had sparked off his anger.

But Celia was unimpressed. 'No, I was forgetting; women do not interest you.'

On the point of an angry retort, Michael remained silent. There was a lull. Celia finished her coffee, patted her lips with her napkin, then spoke conversationally, 'You've finished your cereal, will you have some toast?'

'No, thank you.'

Once more the grey eyes were on him. 'Did you tell the police that you saw her at eight o'clock?'

'No.'

'Why not?'

His boyish face was scarlet once more. 'Well, they didn't ask me and it seemed, well . . . irrelevant.'

Celia shook her head. 'No, Michael! You wouldn't hold back information of that sort without good reason. It was obvious that the police would wish to establish when she was last seen alive.'

Michael looked down at his empty dish and fiddled with the spoon. 'Are you suggesting that I . . . That you think I might have . . .' His voice trailed off.

'Killed the woman? No, I am quite sure that you would be incapable of killing anyone in any circumstances.'

'Well then, I don't see what you are getting at.' Sullen.

Celia poured herself another cup of coffee and added a dash of milk. She was cogitating and, once or twice, she looked across at her brother – thoughtful, speculative.

Michael was staring out of the window through which he could see the tower of his church rising above the trees.

Abruptly, as though the thought had just occurred to her, Celia demanded, 'Was there anyone else in the church at the time?'

'What? – No!'

After a long pause Celia said, 'I'm sorry, Michael, but you are prevaricating, if not actually lying. Either you saw or you have been told something which you are holding back from the police. That is foolish if not dangerous.'

There was a long silence and Michael was on the point of leaving the table when Celia spoke again, 'I had a policewoman here yesterday, while you were in Truro.'

'To see me?'

'No.'

Michael looked the question he was careful not to ask.

'She wanted to consult me about anonymous communications sent to the Dobell woman.'

Michael, already on his feet, sat down again. 'Anonymous communications? What did they say?'

'There were four of them, all quotations from the Bible and concerned with sexual depravity.'

Suddenly Michael had gone very pale. He said with great seriousness, 'The police must have heard something, Celia, otherwise why would they come to you?'

Her expression was smug. 'My work with the Women's Guild is supposed to put me in touch with the women of the village.'

'What did you tell the policewoman?'

'I told her that the fourth communication was not from the same hand as the other three.'

'How could you possibly know that?'

'It was obvious.'

Very carefully, Michael arranged his plate, cup, saucer and spoon. Without looking up he said, 'Recently, Celia, I have begun to feel that I am doing God's work here in Moresk. I thought you shared that feeling.'

'Well?'

'I hope we shan't be forced to move again.'

Celia stood up and began to clear the table. In a tight voice she said: 'Don't forget that it's Tuesday and I have my Fellowship meeting in Truro this morning. I shall catch the ten-twenty bus. Molly Symons has invited me back to her place afterwards so that I may not be home before you go to the Careys' this evening.'

Katherine Geach and Elsa were sitting at the kitchen table, drinking coffee. The old pendulum clock on the wall showed ten minutes past eight.

Katherine seemed to be studying the rings on her fingers. After a moment or two she said, 'I've been a fool, Elsa. Looking back, it's obvious that Abe had been seeing Jessica.'

Caution masked any expression there might have been on Elsa's freckled features. '*Seeing* her?'

Katherine snapped, 'You know exactly what I mean!'

Elsa shifted in her chair, pushed her cup and saucer away, and said, 'I've never heard anything of that sort and most gossip reaches me one way or another.'

But Katherine was not to be put off. 'Don't be difficult, Elsa! The only question in my mind is, when did it start?'

Elsa opened her mouth to reply when Julie came in, fully dressed. On holiday, it was unusual for her to be up before ten.

Katherine vented her annoyance. 'What's the matter with you? Can't you sleep?'

The girl ignored the question. 'Is there any coffee left?'

'In the pot, but you'll have to make your own toast if you want it.'

'I don't want any.'

Her mother's irritation subsided. 'Don't take any notice of me; I'm on edge.'

'I know. I'm going out, but I'll be back around lunch-time.' Julie drank a mug of coffee and a moment later she was gone.

Katherine called after her, 'You should take an anorak or something, it's going to rain.' But there was no response.

Elsa said, 'She looks all in. I didn't think this would have had such an effect on her. I heard her moving about in the night and once I thought she was crying.'

Katherine sighed. 'It's not what happened to Jess that's upsetting her, it's that bloody boy. I wish I knew what was going on there.' She added after a pause: 'I'm not much of a mother.'

Julie walked towards the foreshore and took the path along the river bank. The going was muddy but she picked her way. At the kissing-gate she gave a nervous glance up into the churchyard and hurried past. Her hands were tightly clenched so that her nails bit into the flesh. 'If only I can get him to talk!'

Since overhearing the conversation between her father and the policeman she had felt more than ever troubled and depressed. There were one or two girls at school who talked, glibly, perhaps for effect, of their fathers 'screwing around'. She was not, she told herself, old-fashioned about sex, but she had never thought of her father in that way. She had been naive; for that, apparently, was precisely what he did. And Aunt Jess had been one of his women. Did her mother know – or suspect?

But Aunt Jess had had other men – Giles' father, and the houseboat man, perhaps others. And now she was dead – murdered.

She could not take it in. She thought she had understood how things were at the farm. There was tension and bitterness, Giles had never made any secret of that, and it was obvious to anyone who spent any time at all there. It came about because her aunt seemed to take pleasure in humiliating the Vinters. And yet, despite that, it seemed that she and Giles' father were having sex.

No wonder the police . . . It was like something out of a tabloid newspaper. People would say – must be saying – 'Of course she asked for it!' And they would be speculating about which of her men . . .

But there was something else that troubled her even more deeply. It arose from a casual remark of her father's: 'Henry, down at the post office, says the bits of paper used to wedge the organ keys were cut from a religious magazine which he orders specially for the vicar.'

And it had come to Julie, irritatingly vague but compelling, a memory of having seen such a magazine, curiously mutilated. It was at the farm, but she could not recall exactly where, or in what circumstances.

As she drew level with the houseboat Jumbo came down the gangway with bags slung about his shoulders and carrying a battery of nets. He greeted her with his slow speech, seeming to listen carefully to his own words: 'Hello, Julie! I'm going out to collect spec-i-mens.'

Julie raised her hand but said nothing. She turned up to the farmhouse across the rough grass to the front door, and knocked.

It was opened by Giles. He pushed up his spectacles and regarded her with solemn attention but said nothing.

'I want to talk to you, Giles.'

The boy looked back into the house, hesitated, then closed the door. Still he did not speak.

Julie was at a loss, not at all sure what she wanted to say. In the end it came in the form of a bald question: 'Do you have any idea who killed Aunt Jessica, Giles?'

His blue eyes, enlarged by his spectacles, were cold, indifferent, and when he spoke his voice was toneless. 'What makes you ask me that?'

They were standing, looking towards the river where it was about half-tide. A band of mud separated the shingle from the water and gulls flat-footed around, searching for worms.

'I'm worried, Giles.'

The boy said nothing, he seemed to be staring across the river at the trees which overhung its banks.

Julie went on, 'Have you talked to Michael about it?'

'Why should I talk to Michael?' He sounded bored.

She felt as though she were trying to reach him through a barrier of cotton wool, and she floundered. 'Well, you seem to get on – I mean, it's obvious he likes you.'

Giles flushed and his manner became even more remote. 'I don't know what you mean. What would I have to say to him? Your aunt's death is nothing to do with us.' He added, after a pause, 'Anyway, I haven't seen Michael since before it happened.'

They were silent while Julie gathered her scattered wits to try again. 'Giles . . . Was Aunt Jess out all night sometimes?'

'Yes.'

'Do you know where she spent those nights?'

'It was no business of ours, and I've told the police all I know.'

'The police! Did they question you?'

'I went to them.'

'What did you tell them.'

'I told them something I thought they ought to know.'

Julie was getting nowhere but she was desperate to keep the contact going. 'They say the organ keys were wedged with pieces of paper cut from a religious magazine.'

He looked at her now but his expression did not change: 'So?'

Her courage failed her. She was utterly miserable. 'I don't know. I just wonder what will happen next.'

'That's simple. We shall have to go.' He was wilfully misunderstanding her. 'Your father has sent a man who used to be a farmer; he came yesterday and he's here again today. I expect he will take over.'

Julie was near to tears. 'I'm sorry, Giles. I hope it won't work out like that. I don't think mother . . .' Her voice trailed off because she could not say what she wanted to say with any conviction.

Giles regarded her with a steady gaze and, without raising his voice, in the same monotone as before, he said, 'I don't want to talk about any of this, Julie, and I don't want to talk to you. I would rather you didn't come here any more.' He turned and went into the house, closing the door behind him.

Julie stood, looking at the closed door. In just a couple of days it seemed that her whole world had fallen apart.

Shortly after nine Wycliffe, with his briefcase, presented himself at the front door of Trigg, and was received by the housekeeper, fair and freckled; a youngish woman, plump, and running comfortably to seed.

'Superintendent Wycliffe. I would like a word with Mrs Geach.'

He was shown into the room with the Russian samovar on the sideboard where Kersey had interviewed the contractor. After several minutes, Katherine Geach came in, looking every inch the lady of the house in tailored pale-grey trousers and a matching silk top.

'We can't talk in here, it's like a morgue.'

He followed her along a corridor to a very large room at the side of the house with a bow window which looked out across a lawn to the river.

There were plenty of blue and mauve chintzes, a neutral carpet, sage-green walls with hunting prints, and a white frieze, but Wycliffe's immediate attention was claimed by a grand piano, very much at home in a corner of the room.

'Do sit down, Mr Wycliffe. Would you like something? Coffee? A drink?'

'Thank you, but no.'

She was very pale, doing her best to appear relaxed, but tension showed in the set of her jaw and in her restless hands.

'I'm sorry to return to a subject that must be painful to you but I am anxious to know more of your sister's life.'

She eased the set of her trousers. 'I want to help, but I think you're probably better informed on that subject than I am.' A hint of bitterness.

Wycliffe refused that gambit. 'I'm wondering if you can tell me anything about her association with Jonathan Glynn, and whether she confided in you concerning the accident in which a young boy called Ruse was killed?'

It was not what she had expected and she did not answer at once.

Wycliffe went on, 'I don't wish to probe unnecessarily into your sister's life, but in searching for a motive for what happened I have to look at all the possibilities.'

A quick, troubled look. 'And you think there could be a connection?'

'As I said, I'm merely looking at possibilities.' From his briefcase he brought out Jessica's album. 'If you can bring yourself to look at the last few pages . . .'

She took the album and turned the pages, lingering here and there. When she reached the news cuttings, Wycliffe said, 'Three of those cuttings are concerned with the Ruse family – two with the original hit-and-run, the third with the recent death of the boy's mother.'

She spent some time on the cuttings, then turned back to the photographs. When she finally closed the book and handed it back, her eyes were glistening with tears. She said, 'You obviously know more than you have told me.'

'I know that immediately before her death your sister was considering going to the police with information about the boy's death.'

'I see.' She was shocked. She accepted that the sixteen-year-old tragedy might have traumatically affected Jessica's life, but it had not occurred to her that it could have been the reason for her death.

After an interval, she asked, 'Are you suggesting that—'

Wycliffe cut in with decision. 'I am not suggesting anything; I am seeking information. You must understand that this is only one of many lines of investigation and implies no suspicion of any individual.'

She considered this piece of police doubletalk and tried again. 'After my marriage Jessica and Johnny Glynn became very close. We assumed that they would marry . . . Johnny had a reputation as a bit of a wild man.' Her eyes lost focus as she seemed to relive some incident from the past. 'He drove a farm-truck about the lanes at breakneck speed and everybody expected trouble. Jessica was often with him.'

'Did your sister drive at that time?'

'Jessica never learned to drive. I've often wondered why. At any rate, there was strong feeling against Johnny after the accident but there was no evidence to suggest that he was anywhere near. All I can say is that Jessica was not the same girl afterwards, though I had no idea what it was that might have changed her.'

'She said, in any case, that she was not with Glynn that night.'

'I know.'

'Could it be that she was with someone else?'

Katherine made a despairing gesture. 'How can I possibly know? She talked to me about it, briefly and for the first time, only a day or two before she died . . . I have to admit, she left me with the impression that she was involved.'

'But she said nothing of the person she was with?'

'No.'

Wycliffe returned the album to his briefcase. 'I am sorry to have caused you further distress. I hope that you will keep our conversation to yourself.'

On his feet, he looked across at the piano. 'Are you the pianist?'

A quick smile. 'No, that's Abe's little indulgence. He used to play a lot when he was younger. He's really quite musical.'

She saw him to the door; once more the lady of the house. She even remarked that the primroses were especially beautiful this spring.

Back in his makeshift office, Wycliffe was looking out of the window at a pair of jackdaws perched on a boundary wall. They had their backs to him and, like an old married couple with nothing new to say to each other, they watched the world go by. A herring-gull, yobbo of the strand, alighted a yard from them and the pair edged their way crabwise to a discreet distance but were not otherwise disturbed.

In the back of his mind he was thinking about the Ruse boy and who might have been involved with Jessica Dobell in that hit-and-run. Did it matter to this present case? Was it feasible that having escaped a possible manslaughter charge, all those years ago, the man would resort to murder to avoid exposure now? Of course, although the law might be lenient after such a lapse of time, public opinion would not.

But murder? And murder in such a sensational vein?

Anyway, he would be talking to Tom Reed.

A tap at the door, and Kersey came in. 'Anything from the Lady of the Manor, sir?'

Wycliffe told him, not forgetting the piano.

Kersey was thoughtful. 'Interesting! It could have been friend Geach who took Jess for a ride that night. From the photographs the two couples seem to have been more of a foursome in those days.'

Wycliffe agreed. 'It's possible. It would explain what Jessica said to the Trevena girl; something about not having played fair with her sister and not wanting to cause further hurt – along those lines, anyway.'

Another tap at the door; this time the duty officer. 'The vicar would like a word, sir.'

'Ask him to wait a moment, please.'

Kersey said, 'Ah, the vicar! He's been keeping his head down; perhaps we should have made more use of him. If some of these parsons had their intelligence network computerized it would make Special Branch look like a bunch of amateurs.'

Wycliffe was thinking of Grace Trevena's rather pathetic story about the vicar and the Vinter boy. Put that way it sounded like a Victorian morality tale and perhaps that is what it was. He picked up his telephone. 'Ask Mr Jordan to come in, please.'

He was shocked by the change in the man. His baby face was pale and seemed to have lost its chubbiness. There was a darkness about the eyes and, above all, there was no sign of that smooth manner which seems to come with the collar and provides even the most timid clergyman with a measure of authority.

'Mr Jordan, this is Detective Inspector Kersey. Please sit down.'

The vicar looked at Kersey with obvious misgiving. 'I hope I'm not intruding, but I had to come . . .'

When he was seated he went on, 'It has been on my conscience though I cannot see how anyone can have suffered through my neglect. However, I mustn't try to condone it.' He had been looking down at his hands, now he met Wycliffe's eyes and said, abruptly, 'I was in the church on Saturday evening; I went there to collect my new service book.'

'At what time?'

'It must have been about eight o'clock. After eight, probably.'

Kersey snapped, 'You saw Jessica Dobell?'

'Yes, she was polishing the lectern.' He spoke in a low voice as though making confession.

'Presumably you spoke to her?'

'Something trivial – just a few words. I collected my book and left.'

'Did she seem as usual?' From Wycliffe.

'I think so. She made some remark about the weather – it rained all Saturday evening.'

'Was she alone?'

'I saw no-one with her.'

Kersey spelt out the question emphasizing each word. 'Did you see anyone either going to or coming from the church?'

Jordan hesitated, then, 'I saw no-one.'

Wycliffe said, 'You realize that you were probably the last person to see Jessica Dobell alive – other than her killer?'

He nodded. 'The thought has kept me awake at night.'

'But failed to persuade you to do your obvious duty.' From Kersey.

Wycliffe followed up: 'I cannot understand, Mr Jordan, why you were so reluctant to come forward. You are quite sure that you are concealing nothing else?'

The poor man had never before been subjected to interrogation. His pallor had given way to a deep flush and he was on the verge of breakdown. Wycliffe did not pursue the question.

'I understand that the dead woman visited the church at odd times whenever she thought there might be something in need of attention?'

'Indeed she did. Jessica was most conscientious.'

'I'm thinking of a morning in late December when there was a christening in the afternoon.'

The fresh shock was obvious. There was an interval while Jordan contemplated his plump hands and, when he spoke, his words were barely audible.

'So you know about that?'

'I want your version.'

'It was innocent, but very foolish on my part.'

Wycliffe waited, the fingers of one hand beating a silent tattoo on the desk top. The mild tension he created was more than enough to loosen the vicar's tongue. It was like taking sweets from a child.

'You see, Mr Wycliffe, the boy Giles is not happy at home . . . The situation is very difficult – a family unit living and working with a woman whose background and aspirations are – were – so different. I'm saying nothing against Jessica; she behaved as we all do, according to our lights. But Giles is a complex and sensitive boy, very easily hurt.'

Jordan looked up and was, perhaps, reassured by Wycliffe's bland, attentive manner. 'In short, Giles sometimes came to me to confide his difficulties. On the occasion you refer to he was particularly upset and I was moved by his distress.' The vicar shifted uncomfortably in his chair. 'Foolishly, I put my arm around his shoulders, he rested his head against me and I smoothed his hair. It was at this point that Jessica came in.'

'Are you homosexually inclined, Mr Jordan?'

Jordan looked at Kersey as though he had received a slap in the face. He did not speak for some time but when he did he had decided on a straight answer. 'I will tell you the truth. Since early adolescence my sexual inclinations have been towards my own sex but, with God's help, I have never, in any relationship, allowed my impulses to carry me beyond a simple caress.'

'Did Jessica ever refer to the incident she had witnessed?'

'Not to me, but I heard from Giles that she sometimes taunted him.' Jordan sighed. 'He was, understandably, deeply distressed and bitter.'

Wycliffe was puzzled by the man. It was probable that he had spoken the truth; certainly not the whole truth, but what was he stretching his conscience to conceal?

Probe a little deeper. 'I understand that you subscribe to the *Church Quarterly*.'

'I've done so since shortly after my ordination.'

'It seems that you are the only subscriber in this district.'

'Probably.'

'Are you aware that the folded paper used to wedge the organ keys was cut from a copy of that periodical?'

'I was told so by your officer.'

'How do you dispose of your copies when you have finished with them?'

'I don't dispose of them; I keep them for reference.'

'Will you check to see that you still have the issue for last September?'

The vicar made a little gesture of resignation. 'I have checked; that issue is missing.'

'Can you explain that?'

'I occasionally lend the odd copy to anyone who might be interested in a particular article.' He added, 'It doesn't bother me if they are not returned.'

Kersey interjected, 'You must have some idea who borrowed this particular copy.'

Jordan hesitated then, with obvious reluctance, he said, 'It was the issue which contained an article on the role of the Church in German reunification. Stephanie Vinter happened to see it and said she thought Laurence would like to read it. He is interested in the part played by the Church in the overthrow of Communism in Eastern Europe.'

Wycliffe was gazing at the vicar with disquieting intensity; then abruptly, with a gesture of resignation, he relaxed. What was the point of keeping him on the rack?

But his manner was still brusque. 'I want you to make a further statement about your visit to the church on Saturday evening, and the loan of your magazine to Vinter. At the same time I must remind you that holding back information, however privileged, could delay our investigation and might be dangerous. Somebody who has killed once has broken through a psychological barrier and may well find it easier to kill a second time.'

Wycliffe got to his feet. 'Mr Kersey will show you to the interview room where you will be given the opportunity to make a fresh statement.'

Jordan looked at him, pale and solemn, but said nothing.

Left alone, Wycliffe was still worried by the man. Law enforcement has always had special problems with tender consciences but it is no longer approved procedure to put to the torture their troublesome possessors.

Chapter Nine

Tuesday morning (continued)

When Kersey had taken the vicar to make his statement, Wycliffe left for the houseboat. He went alone, counting more than he cared to admit on the interview with the former biochemist. It was not actually raining but a pearly mist softened outlines with the effect of a lens that is slightly out of focus. The surface of the water was greeny brown, still and shining; it was hard to believe that the tides reached so far. He passed the kissing-gate to the church and, arriving at the reed bed, encountered a troop of bird-watchers, with their binoculars who charmed him with their twittered 'Good morning's.

As he approached the houseboat he could hear music – an orchestra; a radio or record player? Another musician? The orchestra gave way to a single female voice followed by an unaccompanied duet, and at the bottom of the gangway he stood still to listen. The sound seemed to fill the whole valley with trills and cadences which echoed back from the slopes and it was some time before he realized that the bearded Lavin was leaning on the rail looking down at him.

'You like it?'

An indeterminate grunt.

'"The Flower Duet" from *Lakme*, Heady stuff – an aural narcotic not to be taken by policemen.'

'Mr Lavin? Superintendent Wycliffe.'

'You'd better come up.'

On deck a short companionway led down to a saloon which was filled by the music. Lavin switched off the player.

The light, coming from a row of windows near the ceiling, had a greenish hue. Below the windows were aquaria, lined end to end, and below them again, bookshelves and cupboards. There was a bench with an impressive binocular microscope, and another with a sink and rows of bottles.

Lavin stood so that his left side was shielded. He pushed forward a chair for Wycliffe and sat down himself. Certain movements seemed to involve a painful strain. 'What do you want?'

'I am inquiring about Jessica Dobell.'

'She's dead. Your interest has come too late to do much about it.'

Wycliffe was aware of the tension in the man; his whole frame seemed taut, and his manner was aggressive. 'What I can do is to find out who killed her and why. You were on intimate terms with her so you are an important witness.'

'Well?'

'She spent nights here?'

'Occasionally.'

'When did your relationship begin?'

'Our relationship as you call it began five or six months ago.'

'Was it affection, love, or just sex?'

A twisted smile. 'I could ask what the hell that has to do with you.'

'If you answer my questions, Mr Lavin, it will save us both time.'

'All right. I suppose you need to know these things. It was sex – just plain sex.' He seemed to hesitate, then,

'Jessica had no conception of a relationship based on anything other than what was useful or profitable to her. Sex was the area in which I happened to be useful and available. No commitment.'

He looked down at his left hand which was deformed and white with scar tissue. 'I'm not to every woman's taste, but she was titillated . . .' He added at once, 'But I don't want you to think that the arrangement was one-sided. For a man as I am, sex at almost any price must be a plus.'

His head was turned away from Wycliffe so that it was hard to judge his expression.

He added after an interval, 'Poor old Vinter! His sphere of usefulness was on the farm, he didn't quite come up to scratch in bed. Stephanie was no good on the farm and not much use as a housekeeper. And the boy, Giles – the poor lad wasn't much use for anything in Jessica's terms.'

Lavin grimaced as though in sudden pain, and shifted himself in his chair. 'I suspect that there must have been others who passed – or, more likely, failed her tests.'

Wycliffe said, 'So you didn't even like her?'

A short laugh. 'No, I didn't even like her. But I didn't kill her though I'm not totally surprised that someone did.'

'Why do you say that?'

Lavin took time to think. 'There are crude expressions which would answer you precisely but, translated, I suppose one would say that she set out to stimulate a man to the limit of his sexual capacity then disparaged his achievement. Of course that would hardly square with the circumstances of her murder.'

'When did you last see her?'

'Ah!' For once he turned full face, his expression mocking. 'I saw her on Saturday evening when she was on her way to the church. I happened to be on deck as she passed.'

'Did she speak?'

'Casually. Of course, you have only my word for it that I didn't follow her.'

Wycliffe was trying to assimilate what he had been told; it shed fresh light on the dead woman and it also suggested that Lavin had been closer to the Vinters than he had supposed.

'Do the Vinters come here?'

'Laurence drops in for a chat quite often. He's an interesting chap, and knowledgeable; he's keen on natural history and the kind of work we are trying to do here.'

'Did I hear that he's interested in bats?'

'Yes, I believe he's doing a survey of the area for the county records.'

'What about Stephanie and the boy?'

A faint smile. 'Giles looks in occasionally to consult my bird books and he sometimes stays long enough to say "Thank you" when he's found what he wants.' Lavin shrugged. 'He's a strange lad. Recently he's taken to going about with Jumbo on collecting trips. They make an odd pair but they seem to get on, though I suspect that's because of Jumbo's high level of tolerance.'

'And Stephanie?'

A wry look. 'I've never been to bed with Stephanie if that's what you're suggesting.'

'But she comes here?'

'Once in a while, to listen to a new CD if I've got one. Now what free time she has is spent at Trecara with old Carey and his books. The place is falling down about his ears but I gather he's got a good library and Stephanie is helping him to catalogue it.'

'The Vinters seem a very intelligent family; isn't it surprising that they find themselves reduced to the situation on the farm?'

Lavin nodded with emphasis. 'Stephanie's got a first

class brain but she's totally unpractical. When it comes to the nitty-gritty of life she hasn't a clue, and Laurence isn't much better. There's no earthly reason why they should be shacked up here and treated like servants. With a bit of common sense added to their brains they could both land good jobs, whatever Laurence did or didn't do to his wretched student.'

'One more thing, Mr Lavin – the young man who lives here – I don't know his name or his status . . .' Wycliffe was aware of the compulsions which drive policemen to speak with such pomposity but at a loss what to do about it.

A broad grin. 'His name is Mark Wheeler though he prefers Jumbo, and his status is that of a friend. If it wasn't for his reputation – I don't care a damn about mine – I wouldn't bother to tell you that I'm not homosexual. What Jumbo's predilections are I can't say, though I fancy he's a late developer.'

'You came here together?'

'Yes. I was a single man with a decent salary, living just outside Nottingham. I had a house, a boat on the Trent, and a cottage near Newark. Jumbo came to me at eighteen as a sort of odd-job man . . . At the time I thought I might marry and I was preparing the ground.'

A brief pause, then, 'Jumbo doesn't know who his parents were and he's spent most of his life in homes of various sorts. He's too gentle for this world . . . Anyway, I've no close relatives, so we have something in common. We suit each other and when I had my accident it seemed natural what we should stay together. He likes it here and the kind of life we lead; he's becoming quite a good naturalist, all he needs is a bit of theory and the essential jargon.'

'Where is he now?'

'Out with young Giles, actually, getting samples – from the marshy ground around the tower.'

'One more question, Mr Lavin – do you know Arnold Paul, the church organist?'

'I would probably recognize him if I met him but I have never spoken to him.'

Wycliffe was running out of questions; in any case he was only fishing. Before the investigation could take a firm direction he needed to know the victim better, to discover the sources of that hatred which was manifest in the staging of her death.

He thanked Lavin and left. As he reached the bottom of the gangway the music began again. He was impressed by Lavin, he even liked the man. Lavin was ready to admit that he suffered the frustrations of his disability, but he was not perverted by them. It seemed that his self-analysis was sufficiently detached to be objective.

On the other hand Wycliffe was sure that he had not been told more than Lavin wished him to know. A killer? You do not decide on the strength of fifteen minutes conversation whether or not a man is capable of murder. But would Lavin have staged such a tableau? Would, or could Geach have done so? Would Paul? Or, assuming that he had a motive, would or could the egregious Johnny Glynn? Significantly, perhaps, he stopped short of adding Vinter to his catalogue of interrogatives.

It was at this point that a fresh thought occurred to him. As Franks had said, the killer could have been a woman; even a woman of no particular strength. And setting aside, he hoped, any male chauvinist tendencies, he thought he now saw, in the strangely logical yet freakish setting of the crime, more of female than of male psychology. Katherine Geach? Stephanie Vinter? There was no obvious reason why Katherine Geach would want to murder her sister, but the Vinter woman could be a different matter. The Vinters, man and wife, were credible suspects.

* * *

Lucy Lane drove to Truro and contrived to wedge her Escort into a tiny kerbside space somewhere near the offices of Nicholls and Greet in one of the Georgian houses in Lemon Street. Several of the houses in the street hid modern office blocks behind their deceptive façades but Nicholls and Greet practised no such deception; they fitted themselves into the domestic fabric of one of the houses with inconvenience and incongruity, but with consciences clear.

Harry Nicholls' office on the first floor retained its elaborate plaster cornice, its ceiling rose, its deep skirting boards, its multi-paned sash window and elegant panelled door. But, like its occupant, it showed every sign of running gently to seed. Harry Nicholls was fifty, a former scrum-half, now with thinning sandy hair, a high colour, a paunch, and an air of wistful bewilderment.

Lucy felt impelled to be brisk and bright. 'I think you know why I've come.'

The lawyer, concluding that any approach other than a strictly business one would be wasted on this attractive but severe young woman, said, 'The Dobell twins.'

'I understand there was an agreement between the sisters after their parents' death.'

Nicholls fingered a blue file but did not open it. 'Simple enough: ownership of the farm was shared equally between them under their father's will but it was agreed that Jessica should run the place, that Katherine would forgo any claim on the profits and would not be responsible for losses or debts incurred. Katherine's agreement was necessary to any change of use or the disposal of the property.'

'I believe that both sisters made wills at that time.'

'I'm not sure that I should discuss matters involving a living client but, in the circumstances – murder and all that . . . Yes, they made wills each naming the other as sole beneficiary.'

'As far as their interests in the farm were concerned.'

'No, they both used the "all of which I die possessed" formula.'

'One wonders what Katherine's husband thought of that.'

Nicholls shifted around the files on his desk but said nothing.

'Those wills are still valid?'

'As far as I know.'

Lucy stood up. 'Well, thank you for being helpful, Mr Nicholls. I'm sure that what you have told me will be treated with discretion. I can't imagine that the wills are likely to figure in the case but . . .'

'No stone unturned. I know.' Nicholls got up to see her out. 'Do you play golf, Miss Lane?'

'No, why?'

'Or stay at four-star country hotels?'

'Not on my salary.'

'No, so you would hardly be interested in a development which offered such facilities . . .' A bland smile. 'Just a thought.'

He had opened the door for her to pass through. 'Perhaps you will excuse me now, I have another appointment.'

When Lucy returned to her car and a hovering traffic warden, she was thinking that she might have underestimated Harry Nicholls.

Wycliffe continued to walk feeling vaguely guilty because he was enjoying himself. He watched the ducks and the swans, he wondered what species of creature made that rippling arrow-like track on the water, swimming all but submerged, and whether the birds in disturbed flight over the opposite bank were jackdaws or rooks. He thought how pleasant it would be to retire into such a valley, sheltered, perpetually moist, and usually silent. He often imagined withdrawing into such peace and seclusion but rarely thought of what he might do there.

Helen would say, 'You'd be bored within a week; in any case the place is an infallible prescription for rheumatism.'

'Stop the world, I want to get off!' It was a feeling he had often enough, but at other times he was more or less resigned to staying aboard the roller-coaster, screaming with the rest.

But this was a good place. Perhaps a place to die in. Death, he imagined, might come easily, unnoticed, stealing like a mist up the river.

He could see Trecara ahead, a jumble of decaying walls, windows, gables, roofs and chimneys. A low, battlemented wall separated the grounds from the river bank and, as he rounded a bend in the path, he came in sight of an absurd Victorian Gothic gatehouse, now lacking a gate. A car was drawn up there and two men stood by it, talking. One was the whiskered Carey, the other, Abe Geach. Wycliffe was mildly surprised.

They were within a hundred yards of him; they shook hands, Carey turned back to the house and Geach to his car. Geach caught sight of Wycliffe, decided not to see him, then changed his mind and came across the weedy gravel to meet him.

'Good morning, Mr Wycliffe! Finding your way around? Will you let me give you a lift back to the village?'

'No, thanks. I think I'll walk.'

Geach seemed reluctant to leave it at that. 'I've been having a chat with Carey about his house. It's in a terrible state; parts of it could collapse at any time. Pity! It's a fine old place but upkeep is the problem. Trigg is bad enough but this is three times the size and it's been neglected.'

He was talking too much.

'Are you undertaking restoration?'

'Well, it's been talked about, but Carey couldn't run to it. To put that place in good shape would set him back forty grand. It's a difficult building – a rabbit warren.'

'And the rabbits?'

Geach chuckled. 'There's old Carey – though he's not as old as you might think. I'm forty-one and he could give me ten years – no more; then there's his niece, and the Pascoes. The Pascoes, man and wife, must be in their sixties. They started there as servants in Carey's father's time; what they are now, God knows. I doubt if they ever get paid.'

They had come to a halt beside the contractor's car.

'Do the Careys have any friends?'

Geach pouted. 'The vicar is a regular visitor, I believe; and recently Stephanie Vinter. That set a few tongues wagging. She's supposed to be helping him sort out his library so perhaps he's hoping to raise a bit of capital.'

He had his hand on the car door. 'Sure you won't change your mind?'

'Thanks all the same.'

Geach, still uneasy, drove off up the road which was little more than a track. Wycliffe followed him with his eyes, and wondered. Had Geach, newly married, already started to look back over the fence? If it was he who had been with Jessica on the night the Ruse boy was killed, and now, sixteen years later, Jessica had threatened or even hinted at exposure . . . Geach had a great deal to lose.

But the bizarre staging of the crime?

Wycliffe walked up the track, through the pillared order of the larchwood. In a few minutes the ground levelled off and he was clear of the trees. To his right, the folly rose, apparently out of a marsh in which thickets of reeds and rushes were interspersed with scrub willows.

He was tempted to take a closer look, but resisted.

Then, looming ahead, and coming towards him, he saw a bulky figure laden like a Christmas tree. When the two were within a few yards of each other Wycliffe said, 'You must be Jumbo.'

The broad face beamed. 'And you're the policeman. I've seen you pass the boat.'

Wycliffe looked at the nets and at the battery of collecting bottles draped around the lad's neck. 'Mr Lavin told me you were out collecting.'

'Yes, in the marsh. You see, this is a freshwater marsh and Brian thought we ought to compare it with the marshes by the river which are a bit salt – because of the tide. Some of the animals and plants you get up here wouldn't like that, and some you get down there wouldn't like it up here.' His forehead creased in the effort of exposition. 'It's funny; some creatures and some plants are very fussy about how much salt there is but others don't mind much.'

Wycliffe said, 'I thought Giles Vinter was with you.'

Jumbo nodded. 'He was, but he didn't want to go home yet. I expect he's gone to the tower.'

'To the tower?'

'His dad is interested in bats and the tower is one of their roosting places. I think Giles is interested too.'

'Have you always been friendly with Giles?'

'No, only lately. He used to go around with Julie.'

Jumbo had very dark brown eyes and when he was speaking his expression was intent and serious. 'Brian – that's Mr Lavin, thinks that we might be able to write something about the valley and get it printed.'

Had anybody, so far, talked to Jumbo about the crime? He couldn't remember anything in the reports. 'Where were you, Jumbo, the evening Jessica Dobell was killed?'

'I was on the boat.'

'You didn't go out all that evening?'

'No.'

'So you couldn't have seen anybody – say, on the river bank?'

'Oh, I saw Jessica on her way to the church. Brian saw her too; he spoke to her – just said "Hullo" like.' His face clouded. 'That was the last time we saw her.'

'Mr Lavin told me that Jessica used to come to the houseboat sometimes.'

The boy's features went blank. He said: 'Yes.'

'Did you like that?'

A frown. 'I expect she was all right . . . But it wasn't the same when she was there. I don't think I liked her very much.' He added, after a pause. 'She spoilt things.'

Wycliffe went back to his earlier line. 'You saw no-one else on the river bank that evening?'

'Well, I saw Mr Vinter, but that was afterwards.'

'After you saw Jessica – how long afterwards?'

'I don't know really. I was still on deck, just leaning on the rail; it was dark.' He lowered his voice. 'A bit before, Mr and Mrs Vinter was quarrelling. I could hear them. You can hear everything on the river when it's dark. Mr Vinter shouted a bit but Mrs Vinter didn't raise her voice, then I heard the door slam and he went past the boat, but he didn't see me. I think he was upset.'

'Did Mr Lavin see him?'

Jumbo shook his head. 'I don't think so; he was in the cabin, working.'

Wycliffe said, 'I'm keeping you; I expect you want to get home with your specimens.'

Stray ends from other people's lives. A man quarrels with his wife, he walks out and slams the door; it happens all the time. But through a coincidence of time and place this quarrel would occupy Wycliffe and his detectives. If Vinter was ever arrested and charged it would figure in countless documents and records and would appear in the press. In solemn tones, worthy of the Recording Angel, counsel for the prosecution would say, 'Mr Vinter, on that Saturday evening when Jessica Dobell was murdered, you quarrelled with your wife . . .'

Chapter Ten

Tuesday morning (continued)

Wycliffe returned to the Incident Room, thoughtful and morose. Kersey was there.

'Nice walk, sir?' Kersey was nursing a mug of coffee. 'Like some? Potter has set up a snack bar in what used to be the kids' cloakroom.'

A constable went to fetch the coffee and Wycliffe sat astride one of the chairs, resting his arms on the back. 'On Saturday evening, after Jessica left for the church, the Vinters had a quarrel and Vinter took an airing along the river bank in the direction of the church.'

'Where did you get that?'

'The boy who lives on the boat with Lavin; he overheard the quarrel and saw Vinter leave.'

'Reliable?'

'I think so; he's not so stupid as people make out; in fact I don't think he's stupid at all. Uncomplicated, I'd say. Of course, what he's told us doesn't amount to much evidentially, it merely means that Vinter joins the club – Paul and the vicar were both coy about admitting not only that they were out and about on Saturday evening but actually in the church. Geach is supposed to have been working in his mobile office, but who's to say he didn't take a little walk? There's nobody in this case with anything like a respectable alibi except, perhaps, Johnny Glynn who seems to have been at the bar as usual.'

Kersey agreed. 'But, for what it's worth, Fox thinks the wellington boot that made his precious toeprint belonged to Vinter. It's not a hundred per cent, but Fox has the boot and he's getting an expert opinion. Chances are he'll get no more than a probable but even a possible could be a useful lever.'

He put down his coffee cup and lit a cigarette. 'And there are other pointers to the Vinter household. Whoever wrote the fourth anonymous note must have had access to the others in order to imitate their style and content, and choose the same stationery. The notes were sent to the farm, and Stephanie admits having seen one of them. Add to this that the vicar loaned his *Church Quarterly* to Vinter – the one from which the wedges for the organ keys were cut. Things are beginning to gel.'

Wycliffe was less euphoric. 'It would be a pleasant change. Anyway, we'd better have Vinter in for further questioning, on the record. If nothing else, he lied in his statement. I'm seeing Tom Reed this afternoon; if you have Vinter in about four, I'll join you when I can. Anything else?'

'Not much. We've filled in a bit of Lavin's background. He was employed in the research division of British Drugs. He qualified as a medical doctor before taking a post-graduate degree in pharmacology. The firm wanted him to stay on after his accident but he opted to go with an out-of-court settlement of damages. Nothing known against him; he was regarded as something of a boffin and a loner. All sorts of more or less good-humoured jokes about him and his boyfriend.'

While they were talking Lucy Lane arrived.

Wycliffe said 'Get yourself some coffee, Lucy. Potter has set up shop in the cloakroom.'

Lucy went out and came back with her coffee. 'I've talked to Nicholls, the lawyer. What we were told about the wills made by the two sisters is not quite right. According to Nicholls, if either of the two sisters died the other came into everything – not only the deceased's share in the farm.'

Kersey was unimpressed. 'So what? I don't see how it affects things. Of course Kathy gets Jessica's few belongings, whatever they are, but I don't imagine they would constitute a motive for snuffing her sister. Anything else?'

Lucy sipped her coffee. 'I don't know. As I was leaving, Nicholls asked me if I played golf or stayed at four-star hotels.'

Kersey laughed. 'He was winding you up.'

'I'm not so sure. It's occurred to me since that he could have been dropping a hint.'

'Of what?'

'There's been talk from time to time of business groups who want to cash in on Truro's prosperity with an up-market country park – hotel, golf course, swimming pool – that sort of thing. I believe that one or two schemes have already come to grief at the outline planning stage and I wondered if Nicholls was hinting at something of the sort affecting the future of the farm.'

Wycliffe was interested. 'I think you could have something. I happened to see Geach this morning, coming away from Trecara, being seen off by Carey. He seemed over-anxious to tell me that they had been talking about repairs to the house. It wouldn't surprise me if he had some deal in mind which could involve the farm and Carey's property.'

Kersey summed up: 'So the plot thickens as far as Geach is concerned. If he was involved in the RTA which killed the Ruse boy and our Jess was having qualms of conscience, plus the fact that she was being difficult about the farm . . . Well, you could say he was killing two birds with one stone.'

Wycliffe said, 'You have a talent, Doug, for making even your own brand of logic sound like fantasy. But Geach must be taken seriously. It's difficult to see him pursuing a double bluff with the Schumann thing but we know now that, musically, he was probably quite capable of setting it up.'

The three were beginning to loosen up; the atmosphere was coming right. Next door, telephones were bleeping; officers were tapping away at keyboards, nourishing the computer, scratching away in notebooks, or drinking coffee. Files were growing in number and bulk. They had settled in.

Wycliffe said, 'Before we get too bogged down, let's do what I suggested last night; let's try to work out some sort of specification for the criminal.' He turned to Lucy Lane. 'You have first go, Lucy.'

Lucy, taken by surprise, gathered her wits. 'Well, I don't think he's the sort to act on impulse. This crime was thought out in advance, planned, even to the cutting out and folding of the bits of paper to wedge the organ keys. Those bits of paper – so carefully cut, they bother me; the attention to detail for its own sake is obsessive.'

She paused, thoughtful, studying her finger nails. 'But the whole tableau seems to have been worked out beforehand and set up with almost loving care . . . Even the exact extent to which he would undress his victim was calculated. It's as though he got his kicks from brooding on every detail of what he would do. It seems to me that this adds up to a lot of hatred.'

Wycliffe was pleased. 'Good start! Hatred rather than lust?'

'I think so, yes.'

Kersey said, 'You talk about planning, but he didn't bring his own hammer.'

'No, but that makes another point – he knew the church

well enough to know where he could find one, and he avoided using a weapon which might be traced to him. I think he's accustomed to being in the church so that nobody would think twice about seeing him there. He also knows the organ and must have at least an elementary knowledge of music.'

Wycliffe said, 'Right! Your turn, Doug.'

Kersey grimaced. 'This is worse than being in the witness box.' He fished in his pocket for cigarettes and lit one. 'I see him as a twisted bastard, sexually repressed. If he had it in for the woman he could have killed her straight off, no need to set up this charade in order to tell the world that she was a whore.'

He blew out smoke and Lucy fanned herself defensively. 'I'd be inclined to think that at one time he must have been bitten by the religious bug. The whole thing has a rather nasty flavour of self-righteousness: judgement and condemnation . . . Then there's the Mary Magdalene stuff. He knew his Bible; and how many do these days?'

'You don't think the motive for the crime was sexual?'

Kersey screwed up his lined features in uneasy doubt. 'I was afraid you'd ask me that. I mean, there's obviously a strong sexual element but somehow I can't see it as a bloke killing his girlfriend just because she was having it off with somebody else. And yet . . .'

'Go on.'

'I was going to say that I still smell jealousy though somehow not of the woman . . .'

Wycliffe was approving. 'I go along with you there. Is that it?'

Kersey grinned. 'I wouldn't want to upstage you, sir.'

Outside the mists had cleared and the sun was shining. Through the open window they heard the church clock dole out a single stroke.

Wycliffe said, 'One o'clock, we shall be late at the Hopton, but I'd better say my piece.

'You've left me with the difficult bit – the nature of the hatred which seems to underlie this crime. Unless the whole set-up is a deliberate con, this hatred isn't only directed against the victim. She is the focus, but it reaches out to others – to Geach, as shown by the wedged organ keys, to the organist, to the vicar whose church is defiled, and even to the Church itself.'

Wycliffe paused, sitting back in his chair. 'In essence, I agree with both of you, and in particular with Doug's emphasis on jealousy allied to hatred. I can't see this crime simply as murder; it looks to me more like a comprehensive act of revenge and defilement.'

He shuffled some papers on his desk; he was uneasy, and it served him right. He had trapped himself into making some sort of analysis of the vague notions that were in his mind. Ideas, once put into words, demand the gloss of logic and thereafter are set in concrete. But having started, he soldiered on.

'It seems to me that we are dealing with a strangely disturbed personality and, though both of you speak of "he", in my opinion there is more of feminine than masculine psychology behind this crime. It could be that we are looking for a woman. I don't suppose Lucy will agree with that.'

But Lucy did, with reservations. 'You may be right about the psychology, sir, but if you are I don't think it necessarily means that we are dealing with a woman.'

'Perhaps a man in drag,' from Kersey. 'But does all this help to pin down the killer? I mean, is he, she or it on our list?'

Wycliffe said, 'Our next question, obviously. If I had to answer it at this moment, I would say, "No".'

They crossed to the pub for lunch. Carey and his niece

were well ahead with their meal, and today they shared their table with the vicar. From time to time Jordan glanced across at the police table, distinctly uneasy.

Kersey said, 'We're putting him off his lunch.'

By the time the police party had finished the others had already left and Wycliffe approached the landlord for enlightenment. As usual, Johnny was taciturn on the subject of personalities.

'His sister goes to Truro on Tuesdays and he lunches here.'

Stephanie Vinter spread a grubby blue tablecloth over one end of the kitchen table and laid three places with knives, forks and spoons. On the bottled-gas cooker a saucepan simmered, puffing out jets of steam. Stephanie's movements were listless, she was pale, her eyes were red and she had that curiously pinched look about the nostrils which goes with sleepless nights and distress of mind.

The back-door opened and Vinter came in; he'd left his boots outside and was in his stockinged feet. Moving like a sleepwalker, he went to the sink and began to wash.

'How are you getting on out there?' Stephanie spoke as though she were inquiring about some distant undertaking of which she had only hearsay knowledge.

Vinter paused in the act of soaping his arms. 'All right.'

'The man that Geach sent – what's he like?'

'He's called Sandry. He seems a decent sort – doesn't talk much.'

'Did he give you any idea of what they intend to do?'

'He doesn't know any more than we do. He's still employed by Geach and, as far as he knows, he's just helping out on a temporary basis.'

'It can't last.'

'No. Where's Giles?'

'He went out but he'll be back for lunch.' Stephanie put

plates to warm under the grill. 'Oh, there's a letter for you. It's on the dresser.'

Vinter finished washing, dried himself and went over to the dresser. With deliberation he slit open the envelope and unfolded the letter. 'It's from Jessica's lawyers.'

'Read it to me.'

'It says: "In connection with the estate of Miss Jessica Dobell, deceased, I shall be grateful if you will make an early appointment at this office to discuss with me matters arising which are of concern to you."'

'What does it mean?'

'Our marching orders, I suppose. What else?'

As he spoke, Giles came in. The boy stood inside the door, looking first at one parent, then at the other. 'Is something wrong?'

His mother said, 'No, I'm just going to serve out.'

They sat down to their stew in which the carrots were still hard. Stephanie said, 'We shall have to make up our minds; how much notice will they give us?'

Vinter, his fork halfway to his lips, put it down again. 'Let's leave it until I've seen the lawyer.'

Stephanie was about to protest but glanced across at her son and was silent.

Giles watched his parents but said nothing.

When the first course was almost over Vinter spoke to the boy. 'If, when we leave here, it meant you going to another school, how would you feel about it?'

Giles considered the question, then, 'When shall we go?'

'I don't know. We have no tenancy agreement so, as I was saying to your mother, it depends on the lawyers. But if it means another school we must make sure they use the same examining board.'

Stephanie got up from her chair. 'There's baked apple.'

She served the apple and they ate in silence. Suddenly

Giles dropped his spoon with a clatter. There was a fourth chair at the table, unoccupied, and he was looking towards it with his expressionless gaze. He said, in a conversational manner: 'Don't you miss her?'

Wycliffe drove into Truro along the devious lane which is its principal link with points east. Just above the town it blossoms into a dual-carriageway and the descent offers a glimpse of the three spires of Pearson's Gothic revival cathedral. The police station, at the bottom of the slope, by a busy roundabout, escapes being a sixties horror, for which somebody should get a small medal.

Wycliffe parked his car and was received by the desk man. 'Mr Reed is in his office, sir. You know the way?'

Wycliffe did.

They were served with coffee in china cups – with saucers, and Reed said, 'I only get this kind of service during royal visits.'

His little office was separated from the CID room by a glass partition. He fiddled with a little wad of typescript. 'I made a few extracts from the Derek Ruse file and there are one or two photographs . . .

'The date was January 3rd 1976 and the boy was fifteen at the time. At about six-thirty in the evening he was cycling home from the village of Trispen, to Tresillian, after spending the afternoon with a school friend.'

Reed must have spent time he could ill spare getting together his dossier and Wycliffe felt a pang of guilt. But exploring blind alleys is a growth industry.

Reed said, 'Derek Ruse was a popular boy and the case aroused strong feelings – especially when the medical evidence suggested that he might not have been dead when his body was pushed over the hedge into an adjoining field.'

The sun, hidden all the morning, had broken through

and was shining directly into the little office. With a massive forefinger Reed separated his collar from his neck. 'This damned office gets like an oven in the afternoons.'

He selected two photographs and passed them over. The first could have been taken in almost any of the minor lanes in the district; the second showed a field ditch by the side of a low hedge. In the ditch, the boy's crumpled body lay under his bicycle which must have been pushed over on top of him. His glazed eyes seemed to be staring up through the wheel spokes.

Reed said, 'That lane wriggles across country between Trispen and Tresillian, up hill and down dale, and it's barely wide enough for a hearse.' He added, after a pause, 'You see how we found him – that was next morning, and it had deluged with rain all night, washing away any traces there might have been.'

Reed sat back in his chair. 'CID took over, but I was kept on the case. The experts reckoned the bike had been struck higher up than would have been the case with a car, so we concentrated on commercial and farm vehicles. We covered the area for miles around, and got nowhere. Of course we realized there might be no trace of the collision left on a sturdily built vehicle with a good fender.'

He paused and looked at Wycliffe. Reed's baby-blue eyes were possessed of a singular innocence. 'No need to bore you with the details, the point is, names began to be bandied about – one name in particular, Jonathan Selborne Glynn. Johnny may seem tame enough now but he had a name as a tearaway then. His father farmed near Trispen and Johnny used to drive around the lanes, hell-bent, in a clapped out pick-up, usually with his girlfriend—'

'Jessica Dobell.'

Reed nodded. 'You're ahead of me, sir. Anyway, we'd had complaints, so it was natural we should think of him.

He admitted that he'd driven through the lane that evening – alone, he said, but he claimed it was more than an hour after the boy would have reached there on his bike. We might not have taken too much notice of his unsupported word but there were two reliable witnesses who saw him in the lane after half-seven that evening.'

Reed brought out a spotlessly white handkerchief to mop his forehead. 'Even the locals seemed satisfied, but I had my doubts. After the accident he could have driven back home and waited – there are plenty of farm gateways in which he could have turned the truck. All he had to do then was to drive along the lane an hour later and make sure he was seen. I put that to the DI, but of course he wanted evidence which I couldn't find.'

Reed spread his great hands. 'There were other suspects, but none that stood up.'

Wycliffe said, 'Well, all I can tell you is that shortly before her death Jessica Dobell confided in her sister, and in a friend, that she knew who was responsible for the hit-and-run and that she had been involved. She spoke of going to the police to tell what she knew.'

Reed stopped in the act of collecting his papers together. 'Did she mention Glynn?'

'In answer to a question, she said that it definitely wasn't Glynn and she added something else. She said that she wanted to go to the police but that she hadn't played fair with her sister and didn't want to make it worse for her.'

Reed looked at Wycliffe, incredulous. 'That adds up to Abe Geach. God, that would be a turn-up for the book! His name came up. Although he'd recently married her sister, it was rumoured that he'd been seen with Jessica in pubs far enough from home to feel safe. One story had it that he and Johnny had come to blows over the girl. Certainly Abe's Land-Rover was putting on a lot of night mileage at the time but we couldn't get anywhere in that direction.'

Reed massaged his chin until it shone. 'Well, sir! Where do we go from here? Is there a chance of reopening the file? I don't like loose ends even when they're ancient history.'

Wycliffe got up from his chair and walked to the window. For a minute or two he stood looking down at the frenetic gyration of traffic at the roundabout. Panic in the ants' nest.

'At the moment I'm more concerned with Geach as a possible murder suspect.'

Reed nodded. 'I see that – if she threatened him.'

'I'm willing for you to tackle Johnny Glynn in general terms about the hit-and-run. Let him know that he's no longer under suspicion, hint that the case could be reopened, and see what comes of it. No mention of any possible link with the present case. And remember, the new evidence, such as it is, is hearsay. I don't need to tell you that it wouldn't stand up in court.'

Reed said, 'Fair enough. That's all I could expect.'

Chapter Eleven

Tuesday afternoon

When Wycliffe returned to the Incident Room, Vinter was just arriving in a police car. He looked pale and drawn like a man on the edge of collapse.

The little interview cubicle was crowded, with Kersey and Wycliffe on one side of the table and Vinter on the other. On the table between them was a tape recorder and, on the wall, a notice setting out the rights of those undergoing police interrogation. An electric clock clicked the seconds away.

Wycliffe felt sorry for the man and was mildly reassuring. 'This interview is to clear up matters which have come to light since you made your statement, Mr Vinter. You should attach no more and no less importance to it than that.'

Kersey switched on the tape. 'This interview begins at 16.04 hours. Present: Detective Chief Superintendent Wycliffe and Detective Inspector Kersey. If you wish, the interview may be postponed and take place in the presence of your solicitor.'

'I feel in no need of a solicitor.'

Through the window of the little room noises reached them from outside; the occasional sound of cars manoeuvring to pass each other in the narrow street, people exchanging greetings, and gulls in squawking flight.

Wycliffe left the initial questioning to Kersey.

'You didn't tell us in your earlier statement precisely how you came to leave your teaching post.'

There was a pause while Vinter looked from Kersey to Wycliffe and back again, then: 'But now you've found out for yourselves, as I knew you would.'

'You were dismissed following an involvement with a girl student.'

'Technically, I was not dismissed, I was allowed to resign and so preserve my pension rights.'

It was strange. This man was wearing the clothes he wore on the farm – bib-and-brace overalls and a khaki shirt – yet he spoke in a cultivated manner with the precision of an academic. He had been warned of the interview in ample time to change but he had chosen to come in his role as a farm worker.

'Would you say that you are, by nature, a man inclined to violence?'

'I would not. In that instance I was the victim of a rather unpleasant young woman. Of course I am bound to say that, am I not?'

Wycliffe intervened. 'It is your relations with Jessica Dobell which concern us now.'

Vinter was looking down at his bony hands, clasped together on the table top. 'I was employed by her.'

Kersey said, 'But you had sex with her.'

The clasped hands tightened. 'I am not proud of that.'

'Another case of a designing woman?'

Vinter shifted on his chair. 'No, Jessica was highly sexed and I am not a monk.'

'Was your wife aware of the relationship?'

'No.'

Kersey sounded relaxed, understanding. 'Difficult, wasn't it? All together in the same house?'

Vinter seemed to be struggling to explain a situation which he had never before put into words. 'These encounters were casual, spur of the moment affairs . . . They did not take place in the house, but while we were working together – in the fields, the barn – anywhere.'

Kersey said, 'Think carefully how you answer this, Mr Vinter. How did you feel about the woman? Were you fond of her? In love? Were you jealous of her having other men?'

Vinter looked at Kersey in astonishment. 'Why should I be jealous? I wished then, and I wish now, that I'd never seen her. We used each other sexually, that's the simple truth. Most of the time I hated her.' He added, in a low voice, 'But I didn't kill her.'

Neither of the policemen spoke and, after an interval, Vinter went on, 'I put my family in the position in which we found ourselves. I was to blame. We were servants, and Jessica wasn't slow to make us understand that. It wasn't a question of being overworked – I've very little idea of what could reasonably have been expected of us; it was her attitude. She was contemptuous of us for the very reason that we had put ourselves in a position of dependence. She could not understand people who lacked the strength of purpose which she had and her instinct was to humiliate them.'

'You are acquainted with Lavin, the houseboat man?'

Vinter's surprise at the abrupt change of subject was obvious and he answered as though with relief, 'Yes. He's the sort of man I can get on with, but I don't see as much of him as I would like. He is the sort of man I can understand.'

'I believe you have a common interest in natural history.'

'I'm trying to do a little work on the bat population of this area.'

'This means going out early and late?'

'Yes, I visit their known roosting places and try to find others.'

'Is Mr Carey another of your acquaintances?'

Was there a momentary twinge of concern? 'I know him.'

'I believe your wife is a fairly regular visitor at Trecara.'

'She is helping Carey with cataloguing his books.' He added, as an afterthought, but giving it some importance, 'Since he's been on holiday Giles has been going with her.'

It was Wycliffe's turn: 'In your earlier statement, Mr Vinter, you said that you did not leave the farm on Saturday evening.'

Vinter sat forward on his chair and looked directly at Wycliffe. 'That was a lie.'

'So we have discovered. Perhaps we can now have the truth?'

'My wife and I had a row.' A small gesture. 'It doesn't happen often but tension has been growing. I mean, Stephanie wanted us to move in with the Careys – Carey knows how unhappy we have been and he offered us a home for an indefinite period, with no strings . . . This was some time ago . . . I suppose it was very kind of him but what would it make me?' A longish pause, and then: 'The long and short of it is that I can't take his charity. Stephanie says I could help out around the place – earn my keep, but that would be just a façade . . . Anyway, we quarrelled and I stalked out.'

'Where?'

He looked blank. 'I'm sorry, what are you asking?'

'Where did you go? A simple question.'

'Oh, I walked along the river bank to the village, through the village and back by the road. I cooled off.'

'You didn't go into the church?'

Vinter shook his head and spoke in a low voice, 'No, I

didn't go into the church and I didn't see Jessica, but what is the good of me saying so?'

'At what time did you leave the house?'

'I'm not sure, but it would be about nine.'

'Did you see anyone, on the river bank, in the village, or on the road home?'

'There were one or two people about in the square but I didn't speak to anybody.'

'Anybody you recognized.'

'Tommy Noall was chatting to somebody on his garage forecourt but I doubt if he saw me . . .'

'There was silence in the little room; only the electric clock, clicking the seconds away.

'Are you interested in music, Mr Vinter?'

Vinter's blue eyes met Wycliffe's. 'Why don't you ask me if I know enough to have set up the thing on the organ?'

'Do you?'

'Yes, but I didn't do it and I can't make any suggestion as to why anybody would want to.'

'When you left home on Saturday evening what boots or shoes were you wearing?'

Vinter hesitated for a long time and Wycliffe did nothing to hurry him. After one or two false starts, he said, 'I was wearing my wellingtons.'

'You have more than one pair?'

'No.'

'You know that one of those boots is being checked against evidence found in the church?'

'Yes.'

'You have no comment to make on that?'

'No, except that I wasn't there.'

'One more question. I understand that you borrowed a copy of the *Church Quarterly* from the vicar, in which there was an article that interested you. What happened to it?'

'I thought I had returned it.'

'Can you remember the circumstances?'

A long period of hesitation which puzzled Wycliffe, then, 'No, I'm afraid not.'

'It was with pieces of paper cut from that issue that the organ keys were wedged – can you explain that?'

'No, I cannot explain it.'

Wycliffe recited, 'This interview ends at 16.34. It has been recorded and will be transcribed. You will then be asked to read the transcription and to sign it if you agree that it is a correct record.' He switched off the tape.

'And then?'

'You will be free to go but I strongly advise you to think carefully about your walk on Saturday evening and about what happened to that issue of the *Church Quarterly*. Two of my officers will return home with you to make a thorough search of the house for the magazine. I can obtain a warrant, but if you have no objection that will not be necessary.'

'I have no objection.'

Wycliffe returned to his office. He felt confused and depressed. A few minutes later he was rejoined by Kersey.

'So you're letting him go.'

'Yes.'

Kersey blew out his cheeks. 'So what? This is only the third day after all. What can you expect?'

Wycliffe fiddled with the papers on his desk. 'I know all that, Doug, but this woman wasn't found in some lay-by off the motorway; she was murdered in the heart of a small community of which she had been part for her whole life. Her associates are known, her life style is known, and the manner of the crime itself might be expected to point to the killer.'

Kersey said, 'I gather you weren't impressed by Vinter as a candidate.'

Wycliffe did not answer at once, then, 'Whatever I think there isn't enough evidence, material or circumstantial, to hold him, let alone charge him. Above all, there is no obvious motive. As far as I can see, Jessica Dobell's death did nothing to solve the Vinters' problems, it merely precipitated a crisis.'

Kersey persisted. 'So you don't think he's our man?'

'He still could be. For an innocent man, some of his answers were anything but spontaneous or convincing but, if he killed Jessica Dobell, there's a great deal more in all this than has so far surfaced . . . What was it Lucy said? Something to the effect that not much of what goes on inside Vinter shows – seven-tenths submerged. She could be right.'

Wycliffe sat back in his chair. 'When Franks said that we would be up to our necks in trick cyclists before we finished I didn't think it would start with me. But this case isn't going to be settled by studying bits of paper wedged between organ keys and toe marks on the bloody floor.'

It was unusual for Wycliffe to swear, and Kersey took note. 'So what's the agenda?'

'I want you to take Fox and Collis and search the farmhouse. Officially, you're looking for what's left of the vicar's magazine but that gives you an open brief. I've no idea what you might or might not find; that's why I want you there. Obviously if you find anything incriminating you'll act accordingly. Don't go until Vinter has signed his statement, then you can take him with you.'

Left alone, Wycliffe looked at the telephone, hoping that it would ring, and at the door, hoping that it would open. The investigation was losing its way; he had reached the stage of a punter picking winners with a pin. He needed a spot of luck. He trimmed his nails, emptied the little dish which Kersey had used as an ashtray, and tidied his files; placatory gestures to unknown gods.

And they seemed to work. At any rate there was a knock, the door opened and Dixon came in with a pink flimsy. 'Fax from CRO, sir. No record of prints from the Paul premises.'

Down the snake. But no sooner had Dixon returned to his post than the phone rang: 'DI Cox, sir. Met Fraud Squad.'

'Put him through . . . Geoff? This is Charles.' They had been at training school together but Cox had joined the Met and got stuck on the promotion ladder. It was from him that Wycliffe had sought information about the Pauls.

'When you phoned yesterday you mentioned that Arnold Paul, in an off moment, had called his alleged brother "Timmy". It rang a bell but I couldn't think why it should. Anyway it came back to me overnight. Arnold Paul was a witness for the defence in a case against a certain Timothy Raison a few years back. Raison was acquitted on charges of false accounting and misappropriation in a company of which he was managing director. That's history; more to the point, we've got a warrant out against him for jumping bail on fresh charges – perhaps a bit more serious this time. It sounds too much of a coincidence for there to be no connection so I'd like to send a chap down to talk to your friend.'

'Be my guest. But you don't see this Raison as a killer?'

Cox laughed. 'More of a twit. We meet a lot of his sort in our line, not very bright; they wade into trouble without noticing it and their success depends on others being bigger fools than they are. Of course, Raison is very small fry but intelligence isn't a conspicuous feature of the financial world – mostly it's cunning and greed.'

'He must have some sort of hold over Paul.'

'I'll keep you posted.'

The gods had failed him; he wasn't interested in crooked dealings which might or might not involve Arnold Paul.

It was almost six before Wycliffe heard from the searchers.

It was Kersey. 'I'm speaking on the car phone. The house seems to be clean. We did a thorough search. Vinter showed not the slightest interest and refused to monitor what we were at. He went back to his work about the farm. Stephanie didn't turn a hair; she followed us around but made no complaint or comment. It was uncanny.'

'Was the boy, Giles, there?'

'Working at his books on the kitchen table. I gave him the chance to be in on the search of his room but he hardly looked up – just said, "No, thank you."'

'Tuesday is pasty night. Cornish pasties, me han'somes! How's that then? The real thing: plain pastry, chuck steak, sliced potato, turnip and onion; nothing minced, nothing diced.' Johnny, doing his Captain Birds Eye act, seemed his usual self. 'Of course, there's the cold table if you prefer it.'

'How big are your pasties?' from Lucy Lane.

'Two just fit on a ten-inch dinner plate – perfect. But nobody eats more than one, and young women worried about their figures are allowed to leave a bit.'

So pasties it was.

Wycliffe's mind was on Vinter. He was uneasy and all his cop instincts told him that he should have held the man for questioning. He told himself that he would have had to let him go again, but his professional conscience was not appeased. On the other hand . . .

The pasties arrived – golden brown, beautifully 'turned in', with a slot in the top to let the steam out.

Johnny was there. 'My wife makes 'em; that's mainly

why I married her. You can use a knife and fork if you must, but the proper way is to pick 'em up and bite from the end – hold 'em in your table napkin but watch out for the gravy, it's hot.'

Kersey and Lucy Lane took Johnny's advice but Wycliffe, victim of his mother's aspiring gentility, used his knife and fork.

Lucy surrendered when only one-quarter of her pasty remained; the two men had cleared the crumbs. 'That was good!' – Kersey. 'Excellent!' – Wycliffe.

Johnny said, 'No dessert, no coffee, but a cup of tea with milk and sugar; then a walk. That's my recipe to aid digestion after a pasty, but if you don't like it, then there's sodium bi-carb on the house.'

Carey, with a gleeful flourish, laid down six of the seven tiles in his rack – 'H-R-A-T-R-Y. With your P, Jordan, that makes phratry.'

The vicar's smooth brow creased into a frown. 'Phratry?'

'Are you challenging?'

A self-conscious laugh. 'No – I know better than to do anything so rash. It's just that phratry is new to me.'

'It shouldn't be. The word has an excellent pedigree, going back to the Greeks; it means a religious or political division of the people – originally, I believe, based on kinship. Your turn, Alicia.'

Alicia studied her tiles and finally selected three: 'I am adding I-S-E to journal, to make journalise – which will annoy uncle.'

Carey grinned. 'There should be an Officer of State – like the old Public Hangman who burned books – charged with the duty of formally banishing such words from the language.'

They were in one of the few rooms that remained

habitable. It was small, with items of furniture too large for it brought from other parts of the house. Although the room was lit by electricity, the chill of an April evening was kept at bay by a paraffin stove, placed close to the table at which they were seated.

Tuesday evening Scrabble was a regular feature of life at Trecara, with the vicar as guest. For him, it was the social event of his week. The game ran its course with Alicia the winner.

'She has no compunction whatever in profiting from the dregs of the OED,' Carey said. 'Shall we have another game and try to teach her the elements of discrimination?'

Jordan smiled a dutiful smile but it was clear that his thoughts were elsewhere. There was no disguising the fact that he was preoccupied and distressed. He looked towards the window where the curtains remained undrawn against the darkness outside and rain trickled down the window panes. 'I really must get back or Celia will be worried.'

'Why don't you telephone? It's raining hard now but that probably won't last long. Tell her you'll be a bit late.'

The vicar hesitated. 'No, Celia likes to keep to a routine.'

Alicia said, 'I'll get the whisky.'

This too was part of the Tuesday ritual; just the one drink before Jordan left. Alicia went to get it.

Carey said, 'I can see that you are worried, and no wonder; it is a most distressing affair. And so inexplicable!'

Jordan fingered the tiles which he had collected together and boxed. 'I'm at my wit's end. I don't know what to do.'

Carey stroked his beard. 'If it would help to talk . . . ?'

Jordan shook his head. 'It is kind of you, Hector, but it's only with God's help that I shall see this thing through.'

Alicia returned with the drinks tray.

'Ah, Alicia, there you are!'

The two men drank their whisky; Alicia, her orange juice; then Jordan got up to go. He made an effort to sound normal. 'Another Tuesday gone by!'

Carey saw him off at the door. The rain had eased. Jordan said, 'Good night! And thank you, both.'

'Let me lend you a torch.'

'No – really, I don't need one.'

It was dark but in the country it is rarely so dark that one cannot see one's way. The weedy gravelled drive curved gently to the grandiose gatehouse. He felt a little relieved; the companionship, the whisky, and the mere admission of his distress had coloured his mood. Tonight he would pray, and tomorrow would be in God's hands.

The arch was ten or twelve feet wide – wide enough to add a certain dank clamminess to the air beneath it and to intensify the darkness. But he could see the dull gleam on the pool which always formed under the arch when it rained and he kept close to one side to avoid it. Then, suddenly, there was a movement close to him, perhaps he let out a startled cry. He experienced a crushing, pulverizing pain in his head, and then – nothing.

That night Stephanie went early to bed; she was prepared against another bad night with tablets Dr Sparrow had given her. She read a few pages of *Mansfield Park*, her current bedside book. It was long since she had read it and she was surprised to discover that the intervening years had made it possible for her to envy poor Fanny Price. After a few pages she put down the book, swallowed a Mogadon washed down with water, switched off her light and snuggled under the bedclothes. Within a short time she was asleep.

Some time later she was awakened by a sudden breeze

which blew a curtain of rain against her little window. Sleepily, she realized that Laurence had not yet returned from his bat-watching. Nothing unusual in that. Then she noticed the reflection of light coming from Giles' room and called to him, 'Don't stay up reading too late, Giles!'

'No, Mother.'

'Good night, dear.'

'Good night.'

Almost at once his light went out and Stephanie fell asleep once more. Her dreams were confused and several times they brought her to the edge of wakefulness, but she slept on. When she eventually woke it was from a mildly erotic dream, and her hand was between her thighs. She sighed, turned over, and realized that Laurence was still not beside her. It was light, with the pale-grey light of early dawn and it was still raining.

Chapter Twelve

Wednesday morning

Wycliffe awoke, feeling sure that he had been disturbed by some sound and, for a moment or two, unable to recall where he was. Then memory returned and so did the sound – a gentle tapping on his door. He sat up in bed and as he did so the door opened. It was Johnny, the landlord, in shirt and trousers.

'I'm sorry to wake you but Celia Jordan has been on the telephone. She wanted to speak to you personally but I insisted on taking a message . . .'

Celia Jordan? Wycliffe's brain was still clogged with sleep. The vicar's sister, of course. 'Well?'

'She says her brother is missing – that he didn't come home last night.' The landlord spoke with detachment, as though disclaiming all responsibility. 'She's a bit odd sometimes but I thought I'd better pass it on.'

Wycliffe, still coming round, looked at his travelling clock; it was a quarter past six. 'Perhaps you will knock on Mr Kersey's door, and on Miss Lane's, while I get dressed.'

Johnny withdrew. Wycliffe got out of bed and pulled back the curtains. At times in the night he had been aware of heavy rain, now it had given place to drizzle. His room overlooked the square and the creek where the usual pair of swans, padding about on the muddy shore, were the only sign of life.

In his dressing gown he used the pay-phone in the corridor to arrange for a patrol car to call at the vicarage. He was uneasy, apprehensive. He recalled his last words to the vicar: 'Somebody who has killed once has broken through a barrier and may well find it easier to kill a second time.' Pompous, but true. A pity he hadn't listened to himself with greater attention. He had hoped to induce Jordan to tell what he was holding back, but he had failed, and could now be facing the consequence.

Fifteen minutes later, with Kersey and Lucy Lane, he was sipping scalding coffee in Johnny's kitchen. Johnny was still inclined to backtrack. 'This could be a mare's nest. As I said, Celia's queer. I've heard talk that in his last parish – somewhere in Wiltshire – they had to put her away for a time.'

Lucy was sent to the Incident Room while Kersey and Wycliffe drove the short distance to the vicarage. A patrol car was parked outside and they were admitted by a uniformed copper. He reported in a low voice, 'My mate is with her in the sitting room, sir. She says she went to call her brother this morning and found that his bed hadn't been slept in. It seems he had a regular Tuesday evening date at Trecara – with the Careys – and he went last evening as usual. I phoned Carey just now and he says Jordan left there at about half-ten.'

'On foot?'

'Yes.'

'Do you know if he usually went by the road or by the river path?'

'His sister says he went by the road. The footpath doesn't save much between the vicarage and Trecara, and if it's wet or dark, it's difficult.'

Wycliffe said, 'I want you to stay here until relieved. If anything crops up get in touch with DS Lane at the Incident Room.'

Back in the car he and Kersey continued up Church Lane; they passed by the entrance to Jessica's farm, and a moment or two later they were at the top of the long track which led down to the manor house. At one time it must have been a well-maintained drive but now the surface was rutted and pot-holed – facts that were even more apparent in the car than they had been when Wycliffe walked it the day before. The mist was so thick that Kersey was deprived of his first close-up view of the tower, and as they jolted down through the larchwood even the tops of the trees were hidden.

They arrived in the open space before the gatehouse to find Carey waiting for them. His silky hair and beard glistened with drops of moisture.

'He's here.' Carey was deeply distressed and found difficulty in being coherent. 'We found him. Alicia went back to the house to telephone but you must have already left . . .' He passed a hand over his face and beard and seemed surprised to find it wet. 'It doesn't seem possible; I saw him off at the door – watched him go down the drive . . . I can't understand how I didn't hear something . . .'

Wycliffe formally introduced himself and Kersey, then the two detectives moved under the arch where Carey had pointed. The vicar was there, lying in a crumpled heap on the ground. The body lay on its right side, half in and half out of a shallow pool formed by the overnight rain. The cause of death was apparent, a massive injury to the left side of the skull above the ear.

For some reason there was not much blood, but what there was had drained into the blond, fine hair, and trickled in rivulets over the cheeks. Away from the actual wound the undamaged skin was pale and seemed to have shrunk over the bones so that the brow-ridges, nose, and chin were more prominent. The vicar's appearance had aged in death.

Kersey said, 'No theatricals this time; no props.'

Wycliffe nodded. 'Simple panic, by the look of it.'

'He must have known more than was good for him.'

Wycliffe was solemn. 'He certainly knew what we should have known – or at least guessed. But here we are, still in the dark. We've missed something vital, Doug, and this poor devil has had to pay for it.'

Kersey said, 'As far as I'm concerned, there's now only one horse in the race. Jordan must have seen Vinter in or near the church on Saturday evening and—'

Wycliffe, irritable, cut him short. 'Get on the car phone; contact Lucy at the Incident Room, and tell her to notify the sister. Then, the coroner and so on. Franks is still at the address in St Mawes – he's going to moan about this – twice in four days, but that's his problem. I shall be at the house with Carey but let me know when the circus begins to arrive.'

Carey had been standing well away from the two men, indifferent to the drizzling rain; now Wycliffe joined him. 'Perhaps we can go up to the house.' He added, 'This must have been a great shock.'

Carey said, 'I shall be glad to get back; I'm worried about Alicia; she says very little but things affect her deeply.'

Seen at close quarters it was more than ever obvious that successive generations of Careys had altered and added to the original house, each in their own idiosyncratic style. The process had culminated in the Victorian gatehouse, after which, perhaps mercifully, money must have run out. Now Wycliffe was to see the inside.

It was depressing. Carey led him through a bare hall and down a long passage, all stone floored and uncarpeted, into a sitting room at the back of the house.

Carey was agitated. 'Perhaps you will excuse me for a moment; I must find Alicia.'

Wycliffe waited in the little over-furnished room where the light was so poor that it was hard to distinguish any detail in the pictures on the walls. The furniture consisted of large pieces from different periods, presumably collected from rooms that had fallen victim to the progressive decay. He noted the cast-iron grate with its surround of Delft tiles, and the stacked, sawn logs beside it, but there was an oil stove in the middle of the room.

Carey was gone for some time. When he returned he was accompanied by his niece and he had changed his jacket and trousers.

The girl was very pale but composed. She said, 'I've seen you at the Hopton, Mr Wycliffe. I'm sorry to have kept you waiting, it was my fault, I made uncle change into dry clothes.' She turned to her uncle. 'Now you will want to talk – I shall be in the kitchen with Winnie if you want me.' Her manner was that of an affectionate mother with her child.

When she had gone, Wycliffe said, 'Just a few questions, Mr Carey. Jordan was a regular visitor here on Tuesday evenings?'

'Yes. I think he enjoyed those evenings. I know we looked forward to him coming.' He glanced at the table on which there was a Scrabble set. 'We usually played Scrabble.'

'So anyone who knew his habits could expect him to be leaving here at . . . at what time?'

'At about half past ten; that was his time, and that is when he left last night. I saw him to the door and watched him as he walked down the drive . . . It was dark, but a clear night.' Carey brushed his eyes with his hand; they glistened with tears. 'He was a good man, but not a happy one, tortured rather than comforted by his religion.'

'Presumably you neither saw nor heard anything unusual?'

'Nothing.'

'What was your impression of his state of mind?'

Carey frowned. 'Well, as you might expect, the poor man was terribly shocked and distressed by what had happened in his church – by the crime itself, and by its bizarre embellishments.'

Wycliffe waited, and when no more came he said, 'I think you were going to add something.'

Carey looked down at his hands. 'Yes, well, I suppose discretion would be out of place in the circumstances. Jordan had other troubles. Yesterday evening, after we had had our meal and while Alicia was in the kitchen helping Mrs Pascoe with the clearing up, he told me, in confidence, that he suspected his sister of having written the anonymous notes which were found in the dead woman's possession. It seems that she did something very similar in his previous parish with unpleasant though not tragic consequences.' After a momentary pause, Carey added, 'Not that he imagined for a moment that she had any part in the crime itself. There was no question of that.'

'I understand.'

Carey was uncharacteristically restless and troubled. Instead of staring at him Wycliffe chose to look at a portrait of a Carey ancestor which hung over the fireplace. It portrayed a strikingly beautiful young woman with a remarkable resemblance to Alicia.

Carey had followed his gaze. 'Elvira Carey. When she died in childbirth at the age of twenty-four, her husband built the tower to her memory.'

He had had time to recover his self-control though his manner was still uncertain and tentative. 'I have very little to go on, but I feel sure that Jordan's worries went even deeper. Looking back, I can't help wondering if he had some idea of the identity of the killer . . . There was something which he wanted to confide but could not bring himself to do. I feel now that if only I had seemed a little more receptive, if I had been a little more persuasive . . . Of course I had no idea that he was in any way threatened.'

Wycliffe was sympathetic. 'I understand how you feel. I had precisely the same impression – that he was holding something back, but I was reluctant to put pressure on him. Now, of course, I regret that I did not.'

'It distresses you?'

'Of course it does!'

Carey seemed surprised. It seemed a new idea that a policeman might have a conscience in such matters.

The rain had stopped and the skies were clearing. Watery sunshine brought fresh colour and life to the river and its banks, but under the arch of the Victorian gatehouse the preoccupation was with death. There a group of initiates began that sequence of rituals prescribed for the discovery of the dead victim of another's hand.

Dr Sparrow, manifestly grown in self-importance, was there to pronounce life extinct. DS Fox, attended by his acolytes, was there to record every minute aspect of the scene of the crime. Dr Franks, the pathologist, under direction from the coroner, had arrived to take charge of the body and supervise its removal to the mortuary, there to perform his peculiar rites. Screens had been erected to preserve all this from prying eyes, but there were none. Kersey, nominally in charge, was mainly concerned with how soon they would let him get back to the job.

Wycliffe arrived while Franks was still making his preliminary examination. The pathologist got up from his knees, brushing his trousers free of invisible dust – he invariably used a kneeling pad. 'Twice in four days of the only break I've had in months! Do I, in some mysterious way, attract these diversions, Charles? Or do you arrange them for me?'

'Neither. I'm quite sure the poor chap got himself topped just to spoil your holiday. Now, what have you got for me?'

Franks became judicial. 'I could say that the medical evidence is consistent with him having died between ten and eleven last night—'

'Good! And I suppose you could also say that death probably resulted from a blow delivered to the left side of the skull—'

Franks finished for him, 'causing a depressed fracture at the junction of the parietal, sphenoid, and temporal bones.'

'In other words, you've nothing to say that might be useful.'

There was a doorway which gave access to what had once been the gatekeeper's room; now it was stacked with boxes, broken furniture, and old beer crates. From the standpoint of the killer it had been simple. Knowing that the pool would force his victim to walk on that side, all he had to do was to stand back in the doorway and wait.

Franks was stooping over the body, taking another look at the wound. 'Perhaps I could add that from the angle of the depression it seems likely that the assailant was significantly taller than his victim. If I was asked nicely, I'd say he must have been not far short of six feet.'

Kersey looked at Wycliffe. 'Interesting, don't you think, sir?'

Wycliffe pointed into the little room with its store of rubbish. 'Perhaps he stood on a box to give him more clout. He had plenty to choose from.'

Franks laughed. 'You see what he's like when you try to help.'

Fox, hovering now, asked if it was all right to go through the dead man's pockets.

Franks said, 'Enjoy yourself.'

Fox had provided himself with a selection of the regulation tagged plastic bags. He explored the pockets which were sodden down one side. The trouser pockets yielded three pounds eighty-four in coin and a grubby handkerchief. The jacket side pockets were empty except for a raffle ticket and a supermarket receipt, but the two inside breast pockets were more productive: a wallet, a cheque book, a ball-point pen, and an engagement book. The wallet held fifteen pounds in notes, a cheque card, driving licence, and library card.

Wycliffe flipped through the pages of the engagement book then turned to Kersey. 'I want Vinter brought in for further questioning. And to keep the record straight we must organize the troops for another round of inquiries: where was everybody, why, and who saw what.

'Now, Fox: everything here is to be minutely examined. If we are to get any material evidence it must come from here. I'm serious about the possibility of one of those crates being used by the killer to stand on.'

Kersey said, 'Where will you be, sir?'

'Back at the Incident Room, keeping my head down.'

Lucy Lane had returned to the Incident Room after informing Celia of her brother's death and was bringing her notes up to date.

'How did she take it?'

Lucy swept back a stray lock of hair – the only sign that she had been turned out of bed and set to work in fifteen minutes flat. 'I find it hard to believe that she really "took it" at all, sir. That's the most charitable view. At first she said nothing. Then I suggested that it might help to talk and she said, "What about? You tell me that my brother is dead, that he was murdered; oughtn't you to be out with your colleagues looking for his killer? Instead of here, playing at being a social worker."

'As I was leaving, she said, "I must tell the bishop."'

Wycliffe said, 'Perhaps she really believes he's gone to a better place. I must admit it would be a comforting thought.'

He was still in his office, brooding, when his telephone rang. It was Kersey, speaking from the farm. 'I'm using the car phone. It seems that Vinter was out bat-watching last night.' Kersey contrived to make it sound like a perversion. 'And, according to Stephanie he hasn't been home since.'

'Wasn't she concerned?'

'Not so's you'd notice; he's often been away all night it seems. But the point is I've just discovered that the farm-truck is missing. It looks as though he's been back and gone again, this time in the truck.'

'He didn't take it last night?'

'Not according to the boy; he says the truck was still parked in the lane when his father left. I've asked Stephanie to check, and find out whether he took anything else while he was about it. The long and short of it is, sir – he's done a runner.'

Wycliffe did not miss the note of criticism. 'All right; phone in what you've got on him and the truck and I'll have it circulated.'

It was necessary to report to the chief. Oldroyd resisted the temptation to say 'I told you so.' Instead, it was: 'You had to make a decision Charles and, as it happened, you made the wrong one, but it's easy to be wise after the event. Any idea where Vinter might have gone?'

'It's by no means certain that he's gone anywhere.'

Oldroyd took a deep breath. The two men had worked together for many years and outside the office they were good friends. In the office there were frequent differences. 'You're holding back on this one, Charles. I take it you now know who you're after?'

Wycliffe was silent, and the chief prompted, 'Charles?'

'No, sir; I'm by no means sure.'

Oldroyd snapped, 'Then I hope you'll act as though you were.'

Wycliffe had scarcely replaced his phone when it rang again. It was Kersey. 'There's some money missing, sir; just a few pounds they kept for emergencies. Nothing else, according to her ladyship.'

'Cheque book? Credit card?'

'I asked her and she looked at me as though I was talking about the family silver.'

'How are they taking it – she and the boy?'

'Nobody could accuse them of dramatizing the situation.'

'What was he wearing?'

'Overalls. It seems he didn't stop to change.'

'A man in overalls, driving a farm-truck, with only a few pounds in his pocket, isn't likely to be making for sunny Spain. I'll pass you over to Lucy and you can give her the details for circulation. After that I want you back here to arrange a search of the vicar's belongings, in particular of his study and his personal papers . . . His sister? If she interferes she'll be obstructing the inquiry. Handle her tactfully, but no nonsense.'

When he put down the phone Wycliffe got up from his chair and stood, staring out of the window of his little office. Ahead, there was only the boundary wall, but overhead the sky was an intense blue and two seagulls, whiter than white, cruised and planed with effortless ease.

It was always his practice in a murder inquiry to concentrate on the victim, and Jessica's life, like anyone else's, was intimately woven into the pattern of the lives about her. To discover and trace all the threads was impossible; one must select, and he had selected those which seemed significant. They pointed to a limited range of possible suspects. The problem was to match the character of any one of these with the extraordinary circumstances of the crime. He had encouraged the drawing up of some sort of specification for the criminal but the plain fact was that none of the suspects had seemed to fit.

Now, overnight, the vicar had become a second victim and Laurence Vinter a fugitive.

Laurence Vinter . . . A man filled with hatred which could find no single target but nourished itself in the meticulous preparation of a tableau in which a brutal murder was no more than a centrepiece . . . A man who, threatened with exposure, had shown no hesitation in murdering a second time . . .

A tap at the door, which opened just as Wycliffe muttered to himself, 'Nonsense! It's not possible!'

Lucy Lane said, 'I've brought you some coffee, sir.'

And yet Vinter was on the run.

He turned away from the window and, for a moment, it was as though he hardly knew where he was.

'Are you all right, sir?'

He sat at his desk and seemed, suddenly, to relax. 'Yes, I'm fine, Lucy. I've just decided that I can't believe the impossible.'

'You're obviously not as good at it as the Red Queen. Perhaps you should practise more. Anyway, coffee.'

He was being mothered, indulged, and he rather liked it. Drinking his coffee, he said, 'I'm going to the farm amongst other places, Lucy, and I want you with me. Send a crime car with a DC to the farm to await our arrival. Mr Kersey is leaving a uniformed man there. Tell the DC to park in the farmyard for communications purposes.'

A few minutes later they were crossing the square together. News of the vicar's death must have got around but there were few people about. Two women outside the post office watched them go by, solemn faced and silent. There must be a sense of shock; probably a feeling of resentment against the police. Why did they let it happen? Despite all the publicity, fictional and documentary, violent crime, when it strikes home, still arouses an expectation of miracles. By the same token Wycliffe felt a responsibility for his failure to deliver.

The garage man had his head under the bonnet of a car and did not see them.

The tide was in, the creek and river were brimming. Swans and ducks cruised close inshore. Wycliffe and Lucy Lane walked along the river bank, past the kissing-gate to the churchyard, and on towards the houseboat.

Chapter Thirteen

Wednesday morning (continued)

Wycliffe said, 'Lucy, how many bats do you think there are likely to be within, say, a mile radius from here?'

'I've no idea: dozens, I suppose. Scores for all I know. Why?'

'I was just wondering.'

This was the beginning of a strange interlude in the continuing relationship between Wycliffe and his two closest associates. The next few hours would remain in the memories of Lucy Lane and Kersey as the period during which they had lost contact with him, when he neither heeded their opinions nor offered them encouragement or direction.

They were drawing level with the houseboat. No music this morning. The canoe floated astern. Jumbo, his arms resting on the rail, was looking down at them, his expression gloomy.

'Mr Lavin about?'

'He's in the cabin.'

'We'll drop in for a word.'

'You don't think we should be getting on to the farm, sir?'

'No hurry. I want to talk to Lavin about bats.'

Lucy followed Wycliffe up the gangway and Lavin came on deck to meet them.

'You'd better come below.'

In the cabin Lucy looked about her with interest. It was obvious that the routine of the boat had been disturbed. On a small trestle table at the foot of the companionway there was a coffee pot, a couple of used mugs, and eggy plates with crumbs of toast. A door stood open to a tiny cabin aft where there were two bunks with sleeping bags and a blanket or two.

Lavin, eyeing Lucy, was careful to present his uninjured profile. He closed the door on the bunks and found them seats.

Wycliffe said, 'You've heard about Jordan?'

'Yes.'

'May I ask how?'

'Rain or shine I go for a walk along the river bank in the early morning. This morning, as I was approaching Trecara, I met Vinter on his way home. He looked ghastly. I asked him what was up and he pointed back to Trecara, muttering something about the vicar, and hurried past.'

'What time was this?'

'Time? We don't take much count of time but I suppose it must have been between half-six and seven. He was in no state for a chat and he didn't want my company. I walked on and found the police at the gatehouse; they'd just arrived. Carey was there, looking like Marley's ghost, and he told me what had happened. But it was obvious enough; the poor devil was lying half in and half out of a pool of water with his head bashed in.'

'Have you seen Vinter since?'

'I haven't seen anybody. I had half a mind to look in at the farm but Stephanie isn't the sort to welcome visitors in moments of crisis.'

Wycliffe said, 'I came here to ask you about bats.'

'About bats?' Lavin's astonishment was obvious. 'What about them?'

'How many do you think there might be within the area that interests Vinter?'

Lavin shrugged. 'You should ask him. He concerns himself only with the immediate neighbourhood and, on the basis of figures he quoted to me, he's looking at a population of considerably less than a hundred. They seem to be spread over four species, mainly pipistrelles. About a third of them roost in the roof of the old tower, while the rest are scattered over a number of sites: house roofs, barns, an old adit . . . You name it. But what's all this about?'

'I've been wondering what Vinter did during those hours and whole nights when his bats failed to keep him occupied – especially out of season.'

Wycliffe received a quick look from Lucy Lane with whom the coin had dropped.

Lavin too. 'Don't you think you should ask him?'

'I would if I could. Vinter is missing.'

'*Missing*?'

'After seeing you it seems he collected a few pounds cash they happened to have in the house and cleared off – in the farm-truck.'

Lavin was incredulous. 'But that's absurd! You're not suggesting that he had anything to do with what happened to the vicar? The man was upset – distressed.'

'I'm not suggesting anything, Mr Lavin, I'm telling you what happened.'

Lavin was fingering his beard. 'There's something damned odd going on!'

'I agree. I also think that your friendship with Vinter was closer than you or he have led me to believe. Did he often spend the whole or part of the night here?'

There was an interval while Lavin decided how to react. He didn't argue or protest but he chose his words with care. 'I think you should understand how things were at the farm while Jessica was alive. The Vinter family were in an intolerable position, and poor old Laurence could hardly deny that it was he who had got them into it. There was bound to be tension between him and his wife and there was no outlet. It was difficult for them to have a discussion, let alone a row, that wasn't monitored by Jessica. And, above all, however they felt about each other, they had to share a room and a bed . . .'

'So?'

A faint smile. 'You are quite right. Until comparatively recently, Laurence would often spend the whole or part of the night on the floor in this cabin. We kept a mattress, a pillow, and a few blankets always ready for him.'

'He never clashed with Jessica's visits?' It was the first time Lucy had spoken.

Lavin looked at her as though he had just been reminded of her presence. 'Obviously he knew when she was away.'

'But recently he has not come so often?'

'He has not come at all at night. I suspect that he made another arrangement. We never discuss the subject. Of course, he looks in of an evening and at weekends and he knows that he is always welcome when it suits him to come.'

Wycliffe stood up, his manner was brisk. 'Thank you, Mr Lavin, you've told me what I wanted to know.'

Lavin saw them off. At the gangway, he said, 'Vinter is a man with a conscience. As a policeman you must know what a liability that can be.'

The sun was shining, the tide was at flood, there were green reflections in the water and everywhere there was stillness.

As they turned up towards the farmhouse Lucy Lane said: 'Bat-watching as an alibi for spending nights out of his wife's bed . . .'

'What about it?'

'Just the cosy accommodations which are possible between men where women are concerned.'

'And not the other way round?'

'That's our weakness.'

A uniformed constable stood by the front door which was a little open.

'DC Curnow is parked in the yard, sir. I believe there's been a message for you.'

Wycliffe tapped on the door and a woman's voice called, 'Come in!'

Stephanie was in the living room. She stood up as he came in, a book in her hand, a finger marking her place. The book was *Madame Bovary*. 'Have you anything to tell me?'

'I'm afraid not, Mrs Vinter.'

She was pale but otherwise she looked as Wycliffe had first seen her: the straight blonde hair with its meticulous central parting, the blue pinafore frock, and the blouse with a pattern of tiny rosebuds. Her hard blue eyes studied her visitors.

'What will happen when you find him?'

Wycliffe was abrupt. 'That depends on the circumstances. Where is your son?'

'He's up in his room. Do we have to stay here?'

'You are a free agent as long as we know where to find you.'

'Hector Carey has invited us to stay at Trecara until this . . .'

'Until this has blown over?' Wycliffe's tone was like a slap in the face.

She had the grace to look embarrassed. 'It is easy for you to be censorious, Superintendent.' She turned to Lucy Lane. 'You see, don't you? The plucky little woman should stand by her husband in all things.'

Wycliffe looked at her, his grey eyes appraising but also puzzled. 'You believe your husband to be guilty of murder – of double murder, Mrs Vinter?'

She flushed. 'You have no right to ask me that question, Superintendent.'

Still watching her, his eyes grave, Wycliffe said: 'No right at all.'

In the yard, Lucy said, 'You were rough on her, sir.'

'You think so?'

DC Curnow, all six foot three of him, was standing beside his car. 'Mr Kersey wants you to ring him, sir.'

Hens were stalking about the yard, pecking at anything which showed between the cobbles. A man in overalls, presumably Geach's nominee, was brooming out the goat house.

Wycliffe got into the car and phoned Kersey who sounded mildly put out. 'I've had the press here, sir, wanting a statement.'

'What did you tell them?'

'I referred them to the Press Officer at HQ.'

'Good! Is that all?'

'No. Not long after we put out the fax on Vinter there was a call from the Transport police at Truro Station. The truck is in the station car park, standing out like a sore thumb among all the private cars.'

'Did they follow it up?'

'Yes. A man in overalls took a single standard class ticket for Plymouth shortly before the seven twenty-one was due to leave.'

'Any evidence that he boarded the train?'

'They're trying to contact the conductor who checked the tickets. I've been on to Charlie Harris at the Plymouth nick and he's going through the motions.'

'Anything from the vicarage?'

'They've hardly got going, sir. I sent Dixon with a

WPC. I thought she might cope better with Celia.' Kersey added after a pause, 'You seem very laid back about the Vinter angle, sir. I mean, we've got a presumed double murderer on the run—'

'That I let slip through my fingers.' Wycliffe hesitated. 'I understand how you feel, Doug, and I don't want you to be too much involved with the Vinter saga. Then, if the sky falls, you'll be like Macavity.'

'What about him?'

'He wasn't there.'

Wycliffe got out of the car and stood, for a moment or two, looking about him, then he turned to DC Curnow. 'I want you to report back to Mr Kersey. Ask him to see that the constable here is relieved as necessary.'

Then to Lucy Lane. 'We are going to the tower.'

'Curnow could drop us off in the Trecara drive, sir.'

'No.'

They walked along the river bank. The screens were still in place around the gatehouse but there was no sign of activity. They continued up the slope, through the larchwood, and arrived on the marshy plateau without a word spoken. The tower loomed out of the scrub, looking more impressive because of the surrounding plain. They followed a raised, stony path which formed a causeway across the marsh to the door at the base of the tower. The lintel above the door was of slate and deeply incised with an inscription: 'Elvira 1833 – 1857. *Amor aeternus*.'

Lucy said, 'I wonder if he would have put up a monument if she'd died at forty-four instead of twenty-four.'

'You're a cynic, Lucy.'

'I'm a realist where men are concerned.'

The stout door, studded with hand-forged nails, was held fast by a crook in a staple. Wycliffe opened the door and they were faced with a spiral stair which wound upwards around a massive central pillar or giant newel post. As they climbed and made circuits of the pillar they came across small lancet windows through which they had fleeting glimpses over the countryside. Lucy counted sixty-eight steps before they came to another door, blocking their way.

Wycliffe muttered, 'Only a latch-lock.' And to Lucy's surprise he produced a length of stiff wire from his pocket, bent it into shape, and had the door open almost at once. 'My one parlour trick.'

The door opened into a circular room about nine feet in diameter. It was windowless except for a single slit in the circular wall into which someone had wedged a piece of transparent plastic, neatly cut to shape. Beneath the window there was a granite slab supported on pillars, like an altar. There was just enough light to see by.

Lucy said, 'It's a little chapel!'

The floor, swept clean, was tiled in slate and the wall had been decorated with murals but the paint had flaked off leaving only hints of what had once been there. Taking up most of the floor space was a camp bed, a wicker chair, a table with a lamp on it, a small bookcase with three or four shelves, and an oil stove of the old type with a fretted top.

Wycliffe said, as though to himself, 'This is where he does most of his bat-watching.'

Lucy sensed the relief in his voice. 'You expected this?'

'Something like it.'

There were army blankets folded neatly on the mattress, there was even a pillow of sorts. The shelves held several books as well as a tin kettle, a saucepan, a teapot, and a china mug.

Lucy watched while Wycliffe walked very slowly around, looking at everything, taking it in. He seemed to approve of what he saw, and finally he said, 'Do you ever feel you could settle for something like this, Lucy?'

She looked at him in astonishment. 'As a way of life? Starting from here I should end up with a cardboard box, under a bridge.'

Wycliffe nodded. 'You're probably right; it's a slippery slope.'

At last, with seeming reluctance, he said, 'We had no breakfast and if we don't go now, we shall get no lunch.'

'You are not going to search the place – or have it searched?'

'Later.'

They arrived at the Incident Room just as Kersey was leaving for the pub. He was subdued, almost sullen.

'The chief has been trying to contact you, sir. He seemed to be in a bit of a twist.'

'He'll be at lunch now.'

At the Hopton, Johnny Glynn was behind the bar as usual but Wycliffe thought the man gave him a strange look. No doubt Tom Reed had been talking to him.

The table usually occupied by the Careys was empty.

They ate in silence for a while but it wasn't in Kersey's nature either to sustain a grievance or to keep quiet for long. He said, 'Are you going to be around this afternoon, sir?'

'Yes.'

'No reports of any sightings from Plymouth. He must be lying low. In overalls and with hardly any money it can't be easy.'

Wycliffe said nothing and Kersey tried again. 'Fox found muddy footprints on one of the crates in the gatehouse. It looks as though somebody stood on it to get greater clout – as you said. He's taken it away to examine it for possible prints.'

'Good.'

The meal continued in silence and while they were still drinking their coffee Wycliffe got up to leave. 'I shall be in my office.'

Kersey turned to Lucy, half-accusing. 'Are you in on this, whatever it is?'

She told him what she knew.

'What did he mean about me being like Macavity – isn't that the name of his cat?'

Lucy grinned. 'Macavity was T. S. Eliot's Mystery Cat who, whatever feline crime had been committed, always had an alibi. He wasn't there.'

'What a thing it must be, to have an education.'

'You must have heard of the musical – *Cats*.'

'Perhaps. Anyway, it sounded a bit nasty to me.'

'I don't think he intended it that way; he's up to something and he's worried. He doesn't want anybody else involved.'

Kersey grinned. 'In case the sky falls.'

'I suppose so.'

In the afternoon there was a long session on the telephone with the chief. Acrimonious at the start, it ended in a resigned acceptance of a situation that couldn't be changed. 'Well, I hope you're right, Charles. If you're wrong, the media will roast us.' Oldroyd sighed. 'And in a year or two I was hoping to go out, peaceably, with my OBE. Clarice was looking forward to that.'

Oldroyd's prospective OBE was a perennial joke in the two families; so all was not lost.

As Wycliffe dropped the telephone the duty officer came in. 'Johnny Glynn from the Hopton wants a word, sir. He won't talk to anybody else.'

Johnny looked nervous, but determined. 'I could have said my say back at the pub but I don't want my wife involved.'

He sat down, looking about him with curiosity. 'I used to be in here pretty often as a boy, usually to get my backside tanned.'

'You wanted to tell me something, Mr Glynn?'

'Yes. Inspector Reed came to see me this morning. I'm sure you know what about. Anyway, I refused to talk to him.'

Wycliffe said nothing, and Johnny went on, 'I suffered quite a bit of aggro over this business the first time round. I told Reed and his boss at the time that I wasn't involved and that was the truth.'

'I think that is accepted.'

Johnny was flushed; little beads of sweat stood out on his forehead and his gestures were exaggerated. He was well primed. 'I was going to marry Jessica Dobell. It was understood. But she couldn't settle for one man and it was the other man she was with that night . . .' He shook his head. 'That finished me!'

Abruptly, he said, 'Do you mind if I smoke?' He brought out a pack of cigarettes, lit one, and leaned forward, confidentially: 'There's another thing I think you should know. It was Jessica who was driving that night.'

'I understood that she couldn't drive.'

Johnny spread his hands in a helpless gesture. 'The silly bugger was trying to teach her . . . In that lane, with a foot clearance when you're lucky!' He broke off. 'Well, you've got to remember, Mr Wycliffe, we were all a lot younger then – and a bit mad.'

Wycliffe said: 'The other man?'

Johnny sat back in his chair. 'No names, Mr Wycliffe. What I know came out in one hell of a row I had with Jessica at the time. I kept quiet then, when it would have helped me to speak out, and I shan't talk now. I've got my living to get in this village.'

He reached forward to tap ash into Kersey's little bowl.

'I came here because if you knew the facts you might ask yourself what was to be gained by stirring it all up. It was a bad business but there must be a limit. Anyway, this is a private chat – no witnesses, no statement.' He sat back, rather pleased with himself, and waited.

Wycliffe said, 'I've listened to what you have told me.'

Johnny waited a little longer, expecting more, but when no more came he stood up. 'Well, I must be getting back . . .'

At five o'clock Wycliffe went to the post office stores and bought a few things; at six he announced that he would not be in for the evening meal, and telephoned Helen; at six-thirty he set off with a borrowed rucksack slung over his shoulder.

He was in a strange mood, almost one of desperation. He *knew*, but in the absence of material evidence he could not act. And that fool, Vinter . . . One had to sympathize, perhaps admire, but it was wrong, and sure to prove tragically wrong in its consequences. Now he was virtually putting *his* job on the line in behaviour almost as quixotic.

He followed the path along the river bank which for him had acquired a symbolic significance. It was the link binding together the elements in his chain: Trecara with its folly, the farmhouse, the houseboat, the church, Trigg, and the old school which was his base.

In the valley it was already evening, the light had a golden hue and the birds were silent. The tide was running out and there were banks of mud being worked over by the gulls. A tidal creek or inlet is not a single landscape, but a cycle of landscapes following the changing patterns of time and tide.

Somewhere in the woods across the river there was a shot which put up a flight of flustered and flapping pigeons. Looking up into the churchyard, through the kissing-gate, he could see a woman on her knees, tending one of the graves.

There was no-one to be seen on the houseboat but smoke came from the cowled chimney. The farmhouse looked deserted but there would be a uniformed man on duty there somewhere. It was the thing to do, in case Vinter returned to his home. Wycliffe was not in a mood to appreciate the irony of it.

Smoke drifted idly upwards from one of the Trecara chimneys and the screens were still in place at the gatehouse.

He followed the track up through the larchwood and on to the marshy plateau. The tower stood out against a dark, towering cloud mass in the southern sky.

The nearer he got to his goal the more absurd his project seemed. He crossed the causeway, let himself into the tower and climbed the spiral staircase to the locked door. A moment later he was inside, and he felt better. It was considerably darker than it had been in the morning and he could just make out the objects which he knew to be there. He took a torch from his rucksack and swept the room with its beam.

Nothing had changed.

He had planned what he would do. First he would light the lamp and the oil stove. He had assumed that there would be enough paraffin, and there was. Life on his father's farm had taught him something about paraffin and bottled gas. Vinter's lamp was a monster, with twin wicks and a pink glass bowl on a fretted brass stand. It spread a pale but sufficient radiance over the little room. The oil stove did not flare, flicker, or 'yellow' and was soon casting the shadow of its fretted top on the ceiling. The place was becoming cosy.

He emptied his rucksack on to the table: a couple of cans of beer, a piece of cheese, some bread rolls, a bar of chocolate, a bottle of water, and a portable telephone.

Half past seven. He peered through the slit window; the clouds now covered as much of the sky as he could see. Soon it would rain and soon it would be quite dark. In the lamplight the paintings on the wall seemed to acquire increased definition; he could make out trees, a faun, a woman in a flowing gown. He noticed too that the boarded ceiling had been painted at one time but he could make nothing of the design.

There was a hatch which must give access to the dome and, presumably, to the bats. He wondered how Vinter got up there, then realized that the ceiling was low and that by standing on the table, a tall, active man could make it.

He was beginning to feel at home. Sometimes he felt not only that he understood, but that he had some kinship with those who deliberately narrowed their horizons, drew in their tentacles, and retreated from life.

He looked at Vinter's books: biographies, journals and diaries in French, German, and English, and recognized another bond; the attempt to live at second-hand.

He began his search of the room. It was no great task. He found what he was looking for, under the camp bed, in a shallow cardboard box without a lid. The box held Jessica's missing half-wellingtons in a plastic bag, a Bible, the mutilated remains of a *Church Quarterly* magazine, a few sheets of notepaper and some envelopes. He did not handle his finds but left them in the box in full view, on the floor.

He was just in time. There were footsteps on the stairs, slow, weary footsteps. Wycliffe turned down the lamp. It seemed an interminable time before there came a fumbling with the latch-lock and the door opened.

Wycliffe turned up the lamp. 'I was beginning to think you wouldn't come.'

Vinter stood just inside the door, holding on to it as though for support. 'Christ! I might have known.'

He came forward into the room, staggering with fatigue, and slumped into the wicker chair. He looked at the cardboard box with its contents.

'So you found them?'

'Of course; you knew they were there.'

'I put them there, didn't I?'

Wycliffe looked down at him and said, in a tone of mild rebuke, 'Don't play the bloody fool, Vinter, and don't treat me like one.'

Chapter Fourteen

Thursday morning

It was five in the morning, still dark and chilly, when a police car dropped Wycliffe off at the Hopton. He let himself in with the key Johnny had given him. In his room, he undressed, had a quick wash, and got into bed. He told himself that in the next few hours he must be in a position to show that his conclusions were inescapable. '*Inescapable*,' he muttered the word, drowsily – repeatedly, and its syllables seemed to acquire an hypnotic rhythm: in-es-cap-a-ble, so that he fell asleep.

The next thing he knew it was daylight and his little clock showed seven-thirty. He joined Kersey and Lucy Lane in the dining room for the tail end of the eight o'clock radio news.

'It has just been reported that during the night a man attended voluntarily at Truro Police Station in connection with the murders of Jessica Dobell and the Reverend Michael Jordan in the village of Moresk just outside the town. The man has not been named and a spokesman said that he had not been charged with any offence but was helping with inquiries.

'Yesterday, the police issued a description of Laurence Vinter, a farm worker, employed by the murdered woman, and wanted for questioning in connection with the crimes.'

There were several people at breakfast, more than on

any day so far, and Kersey warned, 'Press, on the next table; ears flapping.'

Kersey and Lucy were subdued, conscious of the need to get back into step, but unable to speak of what was uppermost in their minds, so the three dissected their kippers in silence. Even Johnny had his own reasons for keeping away, and it was a relief when Wycliffe said, 'Well, if we are ready . . .'

Outside it was a typical late-April morning with a moist softness in the air and the promise of a warm day.

Kersey went to buy cigarettes and newspapers at the post office and came back grumbling, 'They looked at me like I was Dracula.'

In his office Wycliffe's manner was still detached. 'Anything from the vicar's papers?'

Lucy said, 'I spent most of yesterday afternoon with Curnow and WPC Dash going through them. Apart from his professional records and correspondence, we found only sermon notes and little essays on knotty theological points. Student stuff. I've rarely seen anybody with fewer personal papers; certainly nothing in the nature of a diary.'

Wycliffe seemed resigned. 'It was too much to expect that he made a record of whatever he knew. Why should he?'

Kersey brought the conversation around to Vinter. 'So the official line is that he gave himself up.'

'He *did* give himself up.'

Lucy Lane asked, 'But what persuaded him to come back?'

'He wasn't going anywhere; there was nowhere for him to go. The Plymouth thing was a feint to get us off his back for a while. In fact he went no further than Truro, and spent yesterday skulking around, keeping out of sight as much as possible. He returned to the tower on foot, after dark, with a half-bottle of whisky and a supply of aspirin tablets. I suppose he hoped for the chance to do what he felt he must do, calmly and with a bit of dignity.' Wycliffe sounded oddly defensive.

Kersey looked at him in surprise. 'Suicide! You expected that?'

'Of course I didn't *expect* it!' Wycliffe sounded irritable. 'But after seeing his hideaway in the tower I felt sure that he would come back to it – that was all. I suppose it's what I might have done myself.' He made an apologetic gesture. 'At any rate, I was sure he wasn't stupid enough to go on the run.'

'But why suicide?' From Lucy Lane.

Wycliffe's eyelids were pricking and there was a heaviness at the base of his skull. He could have done with a couple of those aspirins.

'As Vinter saw it, our investigation, if it was allowed to go on, could lead to only one conclusion, and he felt that he couldn't live with the consequences of that.'

Wycliffe had been fiddling with the objects on his desk, arranging and rearranging them. (In stressful times he still missed his pipe.) He looked up. 'I don't know if Vinter loves his wife, he's certainly proud of her, yet it was he who brought on her the humiliations of life on the farm, and he can't forget that.'

Kersey was looking at Wycliffe, his lined features creased even more deeply by doubt. 'I don't know about Lucy, but I'm still at sea.'

'It's simple enough. Vinter intended to offer himself as a nice, tidy, uncomplaining scapegoat and, if he had succeeded, the evidence being what it is, we should have been forced to pack up and go home. You can't prosecute a dead man but you can saddle him with a load of guilt, and Vinter wanted to settle for that. It was my problem to persuade him otherwise. Even now he's biding his time in a police cell waiting to make some damn-fool confession.'

Lucy Lane said, 'But the circumstantial and some material evidence *is* against him.'

'Yes, and there's more in the tower. Fox is up there now, giving the place a thorough going over. In this case evidence likely to incriminate Vinter has been scattered about like confetti.'

He shifted uncomfortably in his chair. 'Although we worked out a specification for our criminal we made no use of it except to agree that it didn't fit any of our suspects. We laid stress on the planning, on the obsessive attention to detail, but we ignored the absence of any identifiable overall purpose. I said something about revenge and defilement but didn't follow it up. The crime was anarchic, not planned to achieve anything, only to disrupt.'

Lucy Lane agreed. 'A disturbed mind reacting to real or imagined frustration.'

Kersey fished in his pocket for cigarettes. 'Soon somebody is going to say "paranoia"; then I shall go.' He lit a cigarette. 'Back to Vinter, I've been reading the transcript, and I must admit there are times when you wonder if he wasn't deliberately landing himself in it, leaving himself open to suspicion. It took him a while to decide what he had on his feet when he walked by the river that night and he finally settled for wellingtons.'

Lucy Lane said, 'So he's shielding either his wife or his son.'

Wycliffe said nothing, and Lucy Lane looked at him with curiosity. 'What exactly happened last night, sir?'

He seemed put out by the question but after a brief hesitation he said, 'We ate some bread and cheese and drank a can of beer.' He gave Lucy a sidelong glance. 'We also talked, but not on the record, and there will be no report. It was two o'clock when I phoned Division, asking them to divert a patrol car.'

He sat back in his chair as though to signal that discussion was over, and turned to Kersey. 'I hope you realize, Doug, that I put myself out on a limb and it was no place for company.'

Kersey looked embarrassed. 'Being out on a limb has never bothered me unduly, sir, but I take your point. I understand.'

'Good. Now, I want you to look after things here and deal with Fox. Lucy and I will be at the farm. Keep me informed of any developments.

'Ready, Lucy?'

They were just leaving when the telephone rang and Wycliffe answered it.

Fox, pleased with himself. 'I've got two possibles, sir: an index finger and thumb of the right hand on one of the boots, and just a suggestion of a thumb on the magazine that needs enhancement. I'm pretty sure, but I'll do a full comparison check back at the nick.'

For once, Wycliffe's heart warmed toward his scenes-of-crime officer. It was not much, but it was something to put in the file.

The media people had lingered over breakfast but now they were gathered around the old school entrance. He pushed through them with a curt, 'No statement!'

Lucy made for his car, still parked in the square, and this time he made no objection. There were unusual numbers of people in the square, gathered in little groups as though they sensed that another act in the drama was about to be played.

As he got into the car he said, 'Of course, this case will never come to court.'

When they were driving out of the square, Lucy said, 'So you've made up your mind.'

'I should have seen it earlier. Instead I talked nonsense about female psychology. It was only on Tuesday evening that I came to terms with the idea. Of course Jordan knew, and I should have guessed as much from his attitude. But by Wednesday morning Jordan was dead, and it was too late.

'I even warned him, without being clear in my own mind what I was warning him about . . . This case has been a shambles from the start, Lucy.'

They drove up Church Lane, past the church, and clear of the houses. Lucy pulled up at the farm entrance and Wycliffe got out to open the rickety gate. The goats were browsing as usual and, in the sunshine, Elvira's tower looked more like a misplaced lighthouse than ever.

Gingerly, Lucy drove down the rutted track to the farmyard entrance and stopped at the second gate. Wycliffe did not get out immediately and Lucy sensed his reluctance.

'How will you handle this one, sir?'

'As gently as possible. Vinter is in custody and we are asking his wife and son to make further statements. That must be our line for the moment. Of course any formal interrogation will be on the record with a lawyer and, perhaps, a psychologist or one of that ilk, sitting in. But I would like a chat beforehand.'

They were still in the car, watching the hens pecking over the cobbles. Vinter's stand-in was tinkering with an ancient tractor. He looked across at them, but showed no particular interest.

Wycliffe pushed open the car door. 'Let's get it over!'

The house door was shut; Wycliffe knocked, but there was no response.

The man with the tractor called to them, 'I haven't seen anybody this morning but you could try around the front.'

They walked around the house to the front door which was slightly open. Wycliffe knocked again with no result so he pushed the door wide and called out. The narrow passage hall was almost blocked by two large suitcases, and by books, tied in bundles and stacked against the wall.

Giles was standing at the far end of the passage looking vague. 'My mother isn't here.' He was not wearing his glasses and his face looked oddly naked and vulnerable.

'It seems you're moving out.'

The boy looked at the cases and the books. 'Yes. Mother is down at Trecara, getting our rooms ready.'

Lucy followed Wycliffe through into the sitting room and the three of them stood facing each other in semi-darkness. The curtains had not been drawn back.

Wycliffe said, 'Perhaps we could have some light.'

Lucy Lane drew back the curtains and the three of them sat down.

Wycliffe said, 'You're not wearing your glasses.'

'No, they fell off, and I stepped on them.'

'Haven't you got a spare pair?'

'Yes, upstairs.'

'Then why not go up and get them?'

The boy sat, hands on his thighs, massaging them in a curious stroking movement that rocked his body to and fro. He was very pale. He said nothing for a time, then, 'No, I'll get them later.'

The rocking movement continued and the blue, unfocused eyes seemed to shut him off from real contact.

Wycliffe said, 'You know that your father is in custody?'

A flicker of the eyelids. 'He is not my father.'

'Not your father?'

'My father died before I was born. He was a famous mathematician. That man is my stepfather.'

'Have you always known this?'

'I have always thought that he could not be my father. He is a stupid man.'

'Very well. Your stepfather wants to confess to the murders of Jessica Dobell and Michael Jordan.'

The rocking movement ceased, but there was no other response. He sat, motionless, his eyes unfocused.

'Do you think your stepfather is guilty of those crimes, Giles?'

The boy clasped his hands tightly together and there was a long silence before he said, 'He deserves to suffer; more than any of them.'

Lucy Lane asked, 'More than Jessica Dobell?'

The blue eyes were turned on her and a hint of a smile trembled on his lips. 'She's dead.'

Wycliffe wondered at the mental deterioration which appeared to have taken place in such a short time. 'Why did you dislike Jessica so much?'

The rocking movement was resumed and he spoke in a harsh voice: 'She was an animal! She tried once to get me to . . .'

Lucy Lane asked, 'What did she try to get you to do?'

'I don't know.'

Lucy tried again, 'Do you disapprove of all people who enjoy sex, Giles?'

The question disturbed him. Two or three times he looked from Lucy to Wycliffe and back again. Finally he shook his head and did not reply.

Wycliffe said, 'I thought you were fond of Julie Geach.'

For the first time Giles raised his voice. 'I don't want to talk about her!' He made oddly defensive movements with his arms as though warding off a blow. 'Her father called me a . . . No, I won't talk about it. I won't!'

Lucy Lane looked across at Wycliffe, a look which asked clearly enough, 'How far do we go with this?'

Lucy was right to sound a warning note, but for him there were other considerations than the Rules of Evidence.

Almost holding his breath, Wycliffe asked, 'Why did you attack Michael Jordan?'

The boy trembled as though in an effort of self-control but he managed to speak calmly, 'I didn't want to hurt him.'

'So why did you?'

The rocking movement recommenced and for some time he did not speak. Then, very quietly and reasonably, he said, 'I set them a puzzle which I knew that nobody could solve . . . I wanted to see what they would do. I wanted to make them suffer and pay for everything . . .'

'And the vicar?'

'He saw me with that woman's boots in the churchyard. I didn't know, but he told me, and he said that I must tell them, that I must go to you.' His hand, resting on his thighs, were squeezing the flesh so tightly that he must have suffered pain. 'He threatened me. He shouldn't have done that . . .'

In the silence that followed, the telephone startled all three of them. Lucy went to answer it. There was a brief exchange, and she replaced the receiver.

'That was Mr Carey; he says that he was expecting your mother earlier this morning but that she hasn't arrived.'

For a while the boy gave no sign that he had heard, then, in a flat voice and looking straight ahead, he said, 'She's upstairs.'

Wycliffe signed to Lucy to stay and started up the stairs.

The door of the Vinters' room was wide open. The curtains were drawn across the little window, but there was enough light to see the form of a woman on the bed. At close quarters he could hear shallow, irregular breathing. He swept back the curtains, letting in the light.

Stephanie Vinter, wearing a dressing gown over her nightdress, was lying across the bed. A good deal of blood had seeped into the honeycomb quilt from a wound in her head, concealed by her hair. As he stood over her she opened her eyes but there was no sign of recognition. She moaned briefly and her eyes closed again.

Wycliffe went to the top of the stairs. 'Ambulance, Lucy! She has a head wound with some loss of blood but she's semi-conscious . . .'

Back in the room he saw on the floor an old-style desk lamp which he remembered as being on the bedside table. Its base was stained with blood. The boy's spectacles lay beside it where they had fallen and been trodden upon.

He turned to find Giles standing in the doorway. 'She isn't dead, is she? . . . I couldn't sleep and when it was getting light I came in to talk to her . . . We sat on the bed, and I told her . . .' He had difficulty with his speech, choking on the words. 'She tried to tell me that I should . . . She said we would go together . . . I couldn't believe it! . . . I was angry and I picked up the lamp and my glasses fell off . . .'

Thursday evening

It was ten-fifteen and the three were sitting at their table in the restaurant after a late snack meal. The kitchen had closed long ago and they were alone in the room. Through the glass doors they could see the usual group of regulars clustered on stools around the bar.

On their table was a bottle of burgundy; Kersey picked it up and held it to the light. 'There's another drink in there. Shall we split it?'

Lucy put a hand over her glass and Wycliffe shook his head.

'All right; mustn't let it go to waste.'

Wycliffe said, 'Vinter was at the hospital with his wife

this afternoon. It seems she's conscious. I wonder what will happen there.'

Lucy said, 'I wonder more what will happen to the boy.'

'It won't be up to us, thank God! And I doubt if the lawyers will have much say. He's spending the next two or three days under observation in the psychiatric ward at the hospital and it's from there that the magistrates will take their cue.'

Kersey finished off the wine. 'Was Vinter the boy's father, or wasn't he?'

Wycliffe yawned behind his hand. 'Does it matter? The trick cyclists will enjoy finding out. But, whether he was or not, the boy's hatred was directed mainly against him.'

Lucy Lane said, 'I'm going to work on Johnny for some more coffee.'

Kersey watched her go. 'She's coming on, that girl.' Which from Kersey was praise indeed.

Wycliffe was twisting his wine glass by the stem, watching the reflections in the bowl. 'It's been an eventful week: two murders, a psychotic teenager in custody and his mother in hospital; the Met investigating the dubious dealings of the church organist and Abe Geach just one step nearer his four-star dream.'

'You sound bitter.'

'Do I?' Wycliffe sat back in his chair. 'Causes seem so disproportionate to their consequences. Just imagine that Vinter hadn't played the fool with his girl student, or that the Ruse boy had set out on his cycle ten minutes earlier, or that Giles Vinter had drawn a different number in the gene raffle, or that almost anything had been just that little bit different . . . It's no wonder Jessica went to a fortune teller.'

Lucy came back. 'Johnny is bringing the coffee. He says there's to be a service of rededication in the church tomorrow morning and that Jessica's funeral will be on Monday afternoon.'

Katherine Geach was sitting up in bed. The clock radio on her bedside table showed a quarter to eleven. The curtains were not drawn and a top window was open to the darkness and the stillness outside. She had a magazine open on her lap but she was not reading, she was looking at herself in the dressing table mirror. Five nights ago her twin sister, Jessica, had been brutally murdered, but here nothing had changed. Had she? She looked in the mirror and felt guilty.

She could hear Abe splashing about in the bathroom. A minute or two later he came in, wearing his dressing gown. He slipped it off and got into bed beside her. After a minute or two his hand reached between her thighs. So far, since Jessica's death, she had refused him.

'Oh, all right.'

He put his arms round her and held her tightly for a while. 'That's my girl! Now let's get that bloody night-dress off.'

In the village of Moresk things were returning to normal.

THE END